CASTAWAY FROM RHODES

JACQUELINE CERVON

CASTAWAY
FROM
RHODES

Translated from the French by
THELMA NIKLAUS

Franklin Watts, Inc. / New York / 1973

Le Naufragé de Rhodes
(Paris, Presses de la Cité, département G.P., 1968)
Castaway from Rhodes
(London, The Bodley Head, 1969)

This book was awarded the French prize, *Le Joie par le livre,* for 1968, the year of its publication in Paris. The prize is given annually to a book published in France, chosen by a jury of young people.

Library of Congress Cataloging in Publication Data

Cervon, Jacqueline.
    Castaway from Rhodes.

    SUMMARY: Washed up on Turkish shores after a storm, a Greek boy becomes friends with a Turkish boy despite the hostilities between their two countries.
    Translation of Le naufragé de Rhodes.
    [1. Prejudices—Fiction. 2. Turkey—Fiction.
3. Friendship—Fiction] I. Title.
PZ7.C325Cas3   [Fic]   73-5680
ISBN 0-531-02638-8

CONTENTS

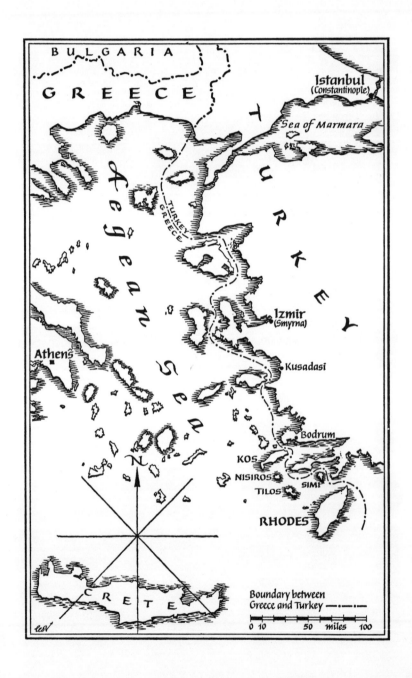

BULGARIA

GREECE

Istanbul
(Constantinople)

TURKEY

Sea of Marmara

Aegean

TURKEY
GREECE

Izmir
(Smyrna)

Kusadasi

Athens

Sea

Bodrum

N

KOS

NISIROS

TILOS

SIMI

RHODES

CRETE

Boundary between
Greece and Turkey ---·---

0 10   50   miles   100

tsN

1

TURHAN

The caique was beating up to windward.

Short tempestuous gusts of wind hurtled against the patched sails; waves crashed over the hull in mounting fury.

Mustafa, his hands locked on the tiller, yelled an order to tack. The men swung the boom round, and the mainsail bellied against the wind. The boat lurched right round in the raging waters.

"We're making no headway at all," shouted Kacim.

"I can't do anything more!" roared Mustafa. "If only that damned engine was working!"

The caique possessed an auxiliary engine and Mustafa relied on this in bad weather. The boat couldn't stand up to sudden squalls, for it was only fit to sail in a fair breeze.

"Might as well have gone on diving," Berduk grumbled in Turhan's ear. "It's not often we find soft sponges!"

"We'll come back," said Turhan, with an effort. He hadn't yet got his breath back. At the end of a working day, after hours of diving, he felt as though he still carried the weight of the sea on his shoulders. His ears were buzzing and his eyes were misted over with spray.

"We'll come back!" grumbled Berduk. "That's easily said.

But by that time the guys from Fetiye will have found the place."

"Why not shelter under the headland until the squall blows over?" Kacim yelled, making his voice carry above the clamor of the howling wind and the waves crashing against the hull.

"Not a hope!" Mustafa shouted back. "We must get to Bodrum and work on that engine. Work all night if you have to. We'll come back to the sponge bed at dawn tomorrow."

There was no argument. On board ship, Mustafa was in charge, and though his crew might be allowed to forget this on a calm day, they were sharply reminded of it whenever it was rough.

Kacim pushed his cap aside to scratch his head. "Tomorrow! . . . Tomorrow! . . . As if you could fix that pump in two minutes! Anyway, while I'm on the job, I want to have a look at the cylinders. I wouldn't be surprised if the valves weren't ready to blow. I told you this engine was giving up long ago!"

"What about you, then? Are you giving up, too?" Mustafa barked at him. "We're going about again, you imbecile. Don't waste time talking!"

"And the sails are rotten," grumbled Kacim. "Everything's rotten in this rotten boat. Sponges, never enough sponges. Never enough, you bet, to spend anything on this old hulk!"

Kacim was the boat's engineer, and he'd performed miracles with the diesel engine that Mustafa had bought cheaply several years back. He regarded the defection of the pump, on the very day of heavy seas, as a personal insult. In his rage, he kicked the wicker basket holding the sticky sponges that made the whole deck reek of chlorine.

"Now then, stop that! Those sponges haven't hurt you!" Berduk shouted.

"They've no right to be there!"

"I'm just going to take them below," said Turhan, struggling to his feet.

"You'd better, if you don't want them sent back where they came from!"

Kacim's temper was as stormy as the sea, but he was right. As the caique rolled, the basket slid from one rail to the other.

"It's blowing colder," Berduk said to Turhan, when the boy came back to sit beside him. "We're really in for it now."

"I don't care," said Turhan. "I could sleep through anything." He stretched out on deck, in the shelter of one of the small dinghies used by the divers. Berduk guffawed with laughter.

"You'll be lucky! All the devils in hell will soon be roaring in those sails."

"Ready about!" Mustafa shouted again from the helm. The boom swung creaking over the heads of Turhan and the other divers lying on the deck. Turhan closed his eyes. The creaking of the sails, the shouting of the men, the lashing of the waves, all these sounds were familiar, for the Mediterranean Sea was often seized with these sudden furies. He was indifferent to whatever might be unusual in the present crisis. Anything to do with the engine or the sails was the responsibility of Kacim and Mustafa. Turhan was concerned only with the sponges, and he had been doing his share of the work since early dawn.

After a hard day's diving, he looked as old at eighteen as Berduk did at more than thirty. Below his curly black hair, his eyes were heavy, his mouth sagged open, and his cheeks were hollow. The other divers also looked older than their years. Only Berduk seemed indestructible. He was a giant of a man, his muscles knotted like ropes, his head set on a short thick neck as round as a mast, his face wide and flat, with a luxuriant black moustache. He and Turhan worked together, and shared one of the dinghies. Turhan exhausted himself trying to keep up with the diving rhythm set by his tough partner.

The sun disappeared beneath a stretch of cloud, skimming the waves. The caique should by this time have reached port and unloaded her cargo of sponges. One of the divers, Husseyin, had spread out his prayer mat on the heaving deck as calmly as if he were in front of the mihrab * of a mosque. He had turned his cap round so that the peak rested on the back of his neck, and was prostrating himself as was right and proper, oblivious of the storm: he was in the hands of Allah.

Two hours later, a wave splashing on his face awoke Turhan from a sleep as deep and dark as a moonless night. He gave a convulsive start and discovered that he was a prisoner. Someone, probably Berduk, had lashed him to the dinghy. The whole crew, sailors and divers alike, were lashed to the caique. Waves were sweeping over the deck. At one moment the bowsprit pointed up towards the dark belly of the clouds; the next moment it plunged into the depths of the ensuing troughs. Clouds were scudding towards the moon, and the caique was racing after them.

Stupefied, Turhan sat up to check the boat's position, to discover that he had made no mistake. The caique was fleeing before the tempest, her mainsail furled on its yard, the jibs close-hauled. Squalls hurled themselves against the one square of sailcloth left. The coast rushed by on the port side.

Turhan became aware of Berduk's great bulk nearby, and called out.

"Hey! Where are we making for at this speed?"

Berduk sniggered.

"We've no choice. The wind is even more pigheaded than Mustafa. It's swung us off course without even asking permission."

---

* Part of a mosque, always in the wall nearest to Mecca, in front of which faithful Moslems prostrate themselves.

"Where's Bodrum?"

"A long way behind us. I've got a sort of premonition that Kacim won't get his pump mended quickly! We'll be spending the night on the skiff . . . or among the Greeks."

Turhan's face was drenched by another wave, and he wiped it with his arm. He spluttered, "Among the Greeks?"

"Where else? Mustafa doesn't know where he's going, even in this direction. And the Greeks are all over the place, on every boulder scattered along the coastline."

Turhan opened his eyes wide to get a better look at the land flying past on the port side.

"But we're not all that far from home. Look!"

Berduk guffawed.

"You're still dreaming, boy! You're not looking at Turkey over there—that's an island, Simi, Greek, of course. To starboard, that's Tilos, Greek, too. And that's not all. Straight ahead, there's Rhodes!"

As Turhan could think of nothing to say in this extraordinary situation, Berduk laughed again and went on,

"We'll be paying a courtesy call on our mates over there. We're already sailing in their waters. They've probably a welcome waiting for us!"

"The coast guards might not be so alert in weather like this," said Turhan.

"I shouldn't be surprised. Anyway, better to watch these waves from a café than the deck of a boat!"

Berduk spat over the rail to emphasize his contempt for the whole race of Greeks.

"There! What did I tell you?" he said, pointing to a land mass looming ahead of the prow, a dark outline between the sea and the sky. "Now boys, what about landing on the famous island of Rhodes? Wouldn't you like to raise the Turkish flag there?"

"I would indeed," said Kacim. "But not today. We'll try to

slip between the island and the Kara headland, and take shelter for the night on our own side."

Whatever Berduk might have to say, Mustafa was still master. Although he had been forced to abandon the idea of beating up to windward, he had not fled blindly before the storm. He had deliberately left Turkish waters, contemptuous of any danger from the Greek coast guards, to find a favorable current. In spite of the great troughs, and the frequent gusts of wind, the caique would inevitably find the current for herself. There could be no question of running ashore on Greek territory: it would be better to sink than to risk that. At the prow, Ismail, a keen-sighted man, was on the look-out for any obstacle, reef or boat, that might loom out of the darkness. He was lashed to the bowsprit, enduring the drenching spray, the crashing waves and the crazy rolling of the boat as if he were a figurehead carved from wood.

All at once the tiller loosened between Mustafa's hands, and he knew that he had won. All he had to do now was to back up the effort the boat was making, and to persuade her as gently as possible to point to the northeast. Now it was a struggle between himself and the wind; but he had strong shoulders, and somewhere beneath the keel he had an ally in the hidden current.

At Cape Kara the ground fell abruptly into the sea, protecting the coastal fringe from the wind that blew from the northwest. The caique lowered her sail and ran on her own headway. Mustafa gave the order to anchor. The sea slapped against the boat in short angry surges, cheated of its share in the wild disorder unleashed that night. Squalls blew high above the mast, which rocked gently against the tangled sky to the rhythm of its own familiar creaking.

Dawn found the men rested and the sea calm.

"Hey, Mustafa! Let's stretch our legs ashore before we leave," begged Berduk.

Encrusted in the headland, like a pearl in an oyster, was a miniature bay bordered with fine sand.

"You coming, guys?"

Some of them, grouped round the pot in which their morning coffee was being made, growled a refusal.

"I'll come," said Turhan, leaping to his feet. His exhaustion of the previous night had gone and he looked himself again, his skin smooth, his eyes clear beneath thick black brows. He busied himself lowering the dinghy he shared with Berduk.

Kacim hesitated a moment before deciding to follow them.

"Why not?" he said. "It'll take the stiffness out of my legs. I'll borrow your dinghy, Husseyin. Anyone coming with me?"

"I'll come," said Husseyin. "But be sure to save some coffee for me, you lot!"

A few minutes later, the two small dinghies had been lowered into the sea that was now mottled with the dancing reflections of the rising sun. The four men descended in turn. Turhan seized the oars. Berduk automatically looked down into the clear water for the gentle undulations of a bed of sponges. Mechanically he stroked the handle of the trident placed beneath the thwart. Turhan rowed, his back turned to the bay.

It was only when their dinghy ran aground that Berduk abandoned his search for sponges, looked up, and noticed a shape stretched out on the sand.

"Looks as though we're not the first to land," he said, surprised.

He shouted towards the second dinghy.

"Hey! Have you seen this?"

"Is it a drowned man?" asked Turhan.

Berduk sneered.

"We can't tell from here, my friend!"

With his ponderous steps he walked towards the body, Turhan following him. The man had been stranded beside a cask that must have served as a buoy to hold him up. He had not had the strength to pull himself out of reach of the water. Waves licked round his legs, and his trousers, alternately swollen and flattened by the water, seemed to be the only thing about him that was alive.

Kacim, with his habitual gesture, began to scratch his head. He leaned over the man, and turned him on to his back.

"He may be alive," he said.

He tried to listen to the man's heart through his soaked shirt, but could not tell whether it was beating.

"He doesn't look dead," he said laconically, and unfastened the shirt to make sure of his diagnosis, revealing a chain round the man's neck, with a cross on the end of it.

"Giaour!" * said Husseyin, kicking the castaway's legs. The cross had arms of equal length; it was a Greek cross.

Berduk looked towards the island of Rhodes, floating in a golden mist on the smooth waters of a peaceful sea. He said with disgust, "A Greek!"

Turhan leaned over, curious to look at a real Greek, a Greek from the opposite coast, not one of those who clung as obstinately to Turkish land as limpets to a rock.

"Greek or not, we'll have to bring him round."

He turned the man over on to his stomach again, put his head to one side, and straddled his back. He did not have to work on his lungs for long. The Greek hiccoughed, spat out some water, and tried to move.

Kacim helped him to sit up. His elbows sagging a little, he straightened his arms and planted them firmly on the sand, so as to support the weight of his body. His head thrown back, the Greek breathed deeply, drawing air into his lungs. After a

---

* "An infidel!": name given by Turks to Christians.

while his head rocked forward, and his eyes met those of the Turks.

All four of them who had helped in his revival were struck with the same amazement: the shipwrecked man was a boy not more than eighteen years old: and he resembled Turhan like a brother.

2

STAVROS

Berduk was the first to react. He slapped Turhan's back hard and shouted, "You never told us you had relatives across the way!"

"But . . . I . . . I . . . I haven't . . ." stammered Turhan.

"Don't give me that! Let's see you side by side." Berduk shoved him closer to the boy they had saved, who was now slowly coming to. As the boy's eyes began to focus properly, he realized he was staring at his own likeness in another's face, as though he were looking in a mirror. It was puzzling, and he lifted one hand to his face to remove the damp sand spattered over it. No doubt about it, he was still himself. His fingers recognized the familiar pattern.

Mechanically, Turhan had made the same gesture, as though he were nothing any more but the reflection of the boy facing him.

"Just look at them!" Berduk laughed. "Was there ever anything like it! They're as alike as two peas in a pod!"

"Good Heavens!" said Kacim, shaken.

"And yet," Husseyin said in his slow voice, "Ismet had but

one son, so far as I know. That's so, isn't it, Turhan? Your father has only daughters, apart from you?"

Turhan turned to the three men. "I've already told you, I don't know this boy," he said impatiently. "How could a Greek belong to my family?"

He could not understand this extraordinary situation. All he knew was that he had nothing whatsoever to do with the Greek.

He held his offending countenance between his two hands, as though to mold it into a shape more distinctively Turkish. Then, just in case he had dreamed it all, he looked across at the shipwrecked boy again, hoping to see on him the sort of ruffian head that all Greeks had, according to common report. But there was no change: the boy was still his living image.

"My name is Stavros Petronides," the Greek said. "Stavros Petronides. You understand?" He thumped himself convincingly on the chest, but he failed to make his intention clear to the four Turks. Then he smiled. His mind was gradually apprehending the oddness of the situation, and he found it comic. For a fleeting moment the likeness disappeared, and the smile gave his face a youthful look that Turhan's would never have again, marked as it was by three years of excessively hard labor.

It was enough to drive the men's uneasiness away.

"It's just as I thought," said Kacim, scratching his head again in perplexity. "We can't understand a single blasted word he says!"

"I was just wondering who'd have enough time to waste learning Greek," said Berduk. He was amused at the idea of anyone being crazy enough to study the hated tongue. The others laughed with him, except for the two boys, who were busy taking stock of each other.

"But that's not the end of it," said Kacim. "What are we going to do with the lad?"

"What do you want to do with him?" growled Berduk, all
his surliness returning. "Leave him where he is. He knows how
to swim, if he wants to go back where he came from!"

"You must be joking! Rhodes is a good ten miles away."

"So what? He managed it last night with his soap box,
didn't he? So he can do it again in the other direction now!"

Kacim shrugged his shoulders.

"He was driven here by the wind and the current." He
turned towards Husseyin, the silent one.

"You there, what do you think about it?"

Husseyin was still wearing his cap with the peak at the
back. He always said that men who wore the peak in front were
trying to hide from the eye of God, because they did not love
the Creator as they should. He, for his part, had no fears on the
subject and always left his face and eyes uncovered.

"I think that Allah brought him here," he said. "There is
no doubt about it."

"And Allah led us to him," Turhan said eagerly, having
finally escaped from the fascination of that other face.

"Now then! Not so fast!" Berduk said. "If I hadn't wanted
to stretch my legs, you wouldn't have come over here at all.
Your twin would have been left to dry out here like a piece of
seaweed."

"You're just wasting time talking." Kacim pulled them up
short. "We'll take him to Bodrum and hand him over to the police. As I see it, that's the only thing to do."

"The police!" The three others spoke with one voice.
Nearly every sensible Turk, having suffered for too long under
a tyrannical police system, believes that anything is better than
the police.

"The police have nothing to do with it," growled Berduk.
"This lad is ours. We found him, we'll keep him."

"Easy to say," said Kacim. "A foreigner, without a passport, and a Greek into the bargain!"

"No need to go around saying he's a Greek. He looks enough like Turhan to be his cousin."

"You'd have to persuade him not to open his mouth then," Kacim objected. "A Turk who only speaks Greek—you must admit you don't often find one!"

"Maybe he's not talkative," Berduk replied, unable to suggest an alternative. They all turned towards the person most concerned, who was still leaning back on his hands. Theirs was obviously just idle talk. If the boy decided to let everyone know that he was a Greek from Rhodes, he could not be prevented. The game would soon be over.

"In any case, what good does it do us to keep quiet about his nationality?" It was Kacim, the wise one, who asked the question.

"Haven't you got *any* imagination?" said Berduk.

Kacim raised his eyebrows.

"Well, what do you want to do with him?" he inquired.

"What I'd do with a trained bear. Make him work and do what I say." Berduk was looking his most mulish.

"We don't use slaves any more," growled Kacim. "Is this a joke, or what?"

"Not altogether. I'd like to have a Greek at hand for the same reason others want a bear on the end of a chain—for the pleasure of watching him long for his liberty!"

"I'm of the same mind," said Husseyin, the silent one. "Allah has placed this boy in our hands to do with him as we want."

It was then that Turhan intervened for the second time.

"Since we'll have to pass him off as a relative of mine, the Greek will be my guest," he said. This meant that Stavros would be granted some sort of sanctuary on Turkish soil. Hospitality is a sacred duty to whoever offers it; and nothing now could ever undo the fact that the offer had been made.

Burduk scowled.

"Better make sure first that he'll go along with the game," he said, turning towards Stavros. There was no reason why he should agree. Whatever Berduk might think, a man is not a bear. The Turks appeared to be deciding his fate, but the Greek alone was master of his future, in spite of the four men who were his self-appointed jailers, and in spite of the police at Bodrum. Some inkling of this stirred in Kacim's mind.

"Better to leave him here," he said. "Now that he's come round, he'll be able to reach one of the villages along the coast, even if he can't swim as far as the island." Let others make the difficult decisions . . .

Stavros looked thoughtfully at the men, guessing that his fate was in jeopardy; the fact amused rather than frightened him. Life was flooding back into his body, and he was recovering his natural curiosity and his love of adventure. Brought up on the old Homeric legends, he saw himself as Ulysses set ashore near the Cyclops. That huge Turk could easily be Polyphemus, yet he had nothing to fear from such a clumsy oaf. He would always be able to find some way of escaping from him.

Stavros had understood the word "police" in the men's discussion, and had sensed their hesitation. He had no more desire than they to tangle with the police, for that would only bring his adventures to a sudden end. They would send him back to Rhodes at the earliest opportunity after they had filled out a few forms. He would lose his fun.

Stavros was in no hurry to return to Rhodes, for he had a year of freedom ahead of him. An orphan of long standing, he owed everything to his uncle, a wealthy ship-owner, who had brought him up, given him a good education, and trained him to become his own right hand, and ultimately his heir, for he had no son. Stavros, like a spirited race-horse, had often jibbed at his training, and it had come to the point where he and his uncle, both nursing the wounds of too-frequent clashes, had reached a compromise. For one year Stavros was to be allowed to live his life entirely as he chose, but he would receive no financial aid.

His instinct had driven him towards the sea, and he had been taken on a fishing-smack for the season. The previous night, still a novice, he had endured his first storm. The sea had won, but Stavros looked forward to taking his revenge. The captain must have shouted "Man overboard!" when the great wave swept over the deck of the *Niki,* carrying away the boy and the cask he had been trying to lash down; and a man lost at sea would be reported when the boat returned to port. So he must let his uncle know that he had been washed ashore on foreign soil. He was free, but not at the price of a silence that would be both deceitful and cruel. That settled, Stavros was at liberty to allow himself a little visit to Turkey. He had an insatiable curiosity, and was particularly interested in this land which had formerly been Greek, and which every Greek still mourns in his heart as a sort of lost paradise. He was also interested in the boy who resembled him so closely. If these men insisted on sending him back to Rhodes, he would give them the slip. He smiled to himself at the thought.

"By God, he's laughing at us!" growled Berduk. "Let's go! Mustafa must think we've been away for a long time!"

He nudged Stavros with his foot, as a sign that he should stand up, and his face showed satisfaction as he saw that the boy understood, and responded with a certain alacrity.

"This is a docile bear," he roared. "Come on, get going!" and he gave him a great thump on the back.

"Easy now!" Kacim advised. "He's only just come round."

"Allah has returned his breath to him, that he may use it," murmured Husseyin.

Berduk laughed, and gave him a friendly slap on the shoulder.

"Allah always thinks the way you do, doesn't he?" he said, and pushed Stavros towards the dinghy.

"It won't be easy to fit three in," he said. "Sit behind him, Turhan."

"I'd better go in front," said Turhan. "Or I won't be able to row."

"Allah has given him two arms, as Husseyin would say. Let him get on with the drudgery for a while."

He put the two oars into the Greek's hands.

"He won't be up to it," Turhan protested.

"Oh, yes, he will. These people are like vipers. The only way of killing them is to bash their heads in."

His voice shook with the violence of his feelings, and Stavros looked at him, a smile touching the corners of his lips. Then he seized the oars, and drew the dinghy smoothly away from the shore, his movements astonishingly firm after his gruelling experience. The livid circle forming round his mouth was the only sign of the effort he was making to betray no weakness.

All at once Turhan took the oars.

"Move over," he said, pushing him to one side. "You're my guest, not my slave!"

He was not really speaking to the Greek, who could not understand him, but indirectly to Berduk, who sniggered.

"He may be your guest," he said. "But he's not mine, nor Kacim's, nor Husseyin's."

His voice threatened, and Turhan made no reply. It took courage to set himself up against Berduk, to whom he was normally as subservient as a slave. Berduk had trained him according to his own methods, and had turned him into a bold diver, a good fisher of sponges. Turhan, who had started when he was fifteen, had never asked nor expected allowances to be made for his youth. He had been the soft wax on which the tyrant had set his seal; and what was more, up to this moment he had been happy under this tyranny, for his was a gentle nature, hardworking and devoted.

It was remarkable that this boy should have found for another the courage that he would never have used on his own behalf; and that other a Greek, a hereditary enemy. He had acted instinctively, and could hardly understand why.

Confused, and already regretting having crossed his teammate for no good reason, he lifted his faithful eyes to Berduk as he rowed with all his strength.

"We'll get back quicker this way," he said. "Mustafa must be waiting for us before he lifts anchor."

When they reached the caique, the two dinghies were greeted with a volley of insults.

"You certainly took your own time!" shouted Mustafa, as soon as he had appeased his anger. "It'll be months before I let you off again, I can tell you!"

Then, as he caught sight of Stavros,

"Who the devil's that? Where did you dig him up?"

"Half dead on the shore," said Berduk. "We brought him back with us because we couldn't think what else to do with him. He's one of Turhan's cousins, tossed ashore by the sea last night."

"So the game has begun," thought Kacim. If he did not speak up immediately, his silence would unite him with the other conspirators. He wished he knew where it would end. Almost anything could be expected with someone like Berduk. Kacim shrugged his shoulders and grumbled away to himself as he hoisted the dinghies aboard. After all, it was nothing to do with him. Since he must, he'd already forgotten that Stavros was Greek. He'd even forgotten that the sea had flung the boy ashore. He was only concerned with the engine, the leaking pump, and the valves ready to blow; that was enough trouble for any man. If Berduk wanted to make more, that was his affair.

Thus Stavros lost the only ally he might have had among them, for Kacim's judgment carried weight.

As Stavros set foot on deck, Mustafa cried out, "Bless my soul! You certainly do look like your cousin! It's unbelievable!"

"Don't tire yourself out!" said Berduk, winking at his accomplices. "He doesn't understand a word outside his own dialect. We'll have to teach him Turkish, just as if he'd come from the shores opposite!"

Pleased with his joke, he let out his usual bellow of laughter.

"If Allah will permit . . ." murmured Husseyin, which doubled Berduk's noisy enjoyment.

"Good," said Mustafa, disconcerted by laughter he could not share. "Since that's the way it is, you'd better look after your cousin, Turhan. Now let's get going. Anchor aweigh!"

Stavros had quickly understood what was going on, for no Greek would be treated with such indifference by a Turk. He guessed that the four men had taken advantage of his likeness to one of their number to conceal his nationality, and Stavros was more than willing to go along with this. In fact, he found it all rather amusing, and he was smiling at the thought, just as Mustafa looked at him.

"That boy doesn't seem normal," Mustafa growled into his moustache. "Standing there laughing to himself! What about, I should like to know. He must have swallowed too much sea water last night. It's sent him out of his mind."

Having reached this conclusion, he dismissed Stavros from his mind, for they were about to set sail, and there were other things to think of.

Men sprang into activity pulling on the main halyard; the anchor rose from the water. Mustafa took the helm. The sails bellied in the wind, and the caique skimmed along, splendidly forgetful of her damaged engine and patched canvas, sailing into a morning in which the world seemed reborn beneath the sun, between the sky stretched like tented silk, and the dappled sea.

3

BODRUM

In spite of all Kacim's protests and his reiterated demands for an immediate return home so that he could repair the engine, it was decided that they would anchor off the sponge bed. It would be ridiculous to give up a day's fishing, particularly since the caique could only return by sailing through the waters she had left so unwillingly the previous day. Kacim could begin to dismantle the engine, using the boat's tools; and further provisions would be taken on board at Datca, one of the coastal villages.

The men, paired off in their dinghies, dispersed along the bed, which was marked by a wide green translucent streak on the deep blue of the sea, and the divers went into action.

Stavros watched them for a while, leaning on the rail. His enthusiasm had drained away. Perhaps because of his weariness he was beginning to feel sorry that he had accepted the adventure, but it was now too late to draw back. A little earlier, when the caique had been sailing off Simi, he could have escaped and swum to the island, but now Simi was far behind. Mustafa and Kacim, the only men remaining on board, ignored him. He curled up by a coil of rope, overcome with exhaustion. Maybe he would have drowned before he reached the shores of

Simi. He shut his eyes, lulled by the slapping of the waves against the hull.

He wondered what his uncle would have said if he could have seen him on his way to Asia Minor. He had been about the same age as Stavros when he and all his family, including his young brother, the father of Stavros, had been driven out of Turkey, with about two million other Greek settlers on the Turkish coast of the Aegean Sea. He always spoke of that exodus with a bitterness that had not lessened with the passing years.

It was in 1922 that the vast Ottoman empire, which had for centuries extended over North Africa, Egypt, Arabia, the Balkans, and the Near East, had been dismantled after the end of the First World War, and reduced to the single Anatolian plateau, modern Turkey.

Mustafa Kemal, known as Ataturk, the father of the Turks, was the man who had undertaken to make that area, the last bastion of his people, into a powerful modern state. He turned his back on Islam, adopted revolutionary tactics, gave his people a calendar, a metric system, an alphabet and a civil status that were all determinedly European, and emancipated the women, giving them equality and the right to vote.

He also, in his own words, separated the wheat from the chaff, by driving the Greeks from the coastal provinces where they had established their colonies, and by recalling to Turkish territory his forgotten people, scattered in countries that had just escaped from Ottoman rule.

Kemal achieved his enormous task with a ruthlessness bordering on cruelty. Since then, forty years had gone by, but his work remained. The cruelties were forgotten, particularly by those who had not suffered directly. Stavros' uncle had not forgotten, but he was not a man embittered by hatred. He had pleasant memories of his life in Smyrna before the events of 1922. He had told his nephew the salient facts objectively, even going so far as to emphasize that in peacetime the Turks often forgot their racial prejudices to the point of contracting mixed marriages. Turks had been known to marry Greek women.

So Stavros' thoughts wandered, as he relaxed against the coil of rope. His mind, half asleep, lingered on that last idea: Turks had been known to marry Greek women. Maybe he, Stavros, and this boy who looked so like him, shared a grandmother who had passed on her features to them through the generations. The idea was an agreeable one.

Satisfied that he had found an explanation for what had seemed so inexplicable, Stavros sank into a deep sleep and did not hear the divers return for their noon break.

Turhan went over to him, intending to share his hunk of bread and ewe's cheese, and discovered that the Greek was asleep. Mouthful by mouthful, he ate his whole ration, anxious to build up his strength again. Never before had Berduk given him such a hard time. It was almost as though he'd taken him for the Greek, and Turhan had been made to suffer for him. In fact, even before the break he felt as though he had reached the end of his endurance, but there was no point in complaining. Berduk had no pity.

Stavros slept, his head flung back against the coil of rope. His gold chain shone in the sun at the opening of his shirt. Automatically Turhan drew the collar together, to hide that compromising glitter. Someone behind him sniggered. Berduk had noticed.

"What about changing places with him this afternoon?" the huge Turk suggested, his voice unusually gentle. Turhan shivered. Twice as he surfaced that morning, he had caught a dangerous gleam in Berduk's eyes. It was not difficult to finish off a diver: a grip holding him under water just a few seconds too long, instead of a hand stretched out to help.

"That's agreed, then?" Berduk insisted.

Turhan shook his head.

"He probably doesn't know how to dive. It'd mean a whole afternoon lost. If Kacim's right about having to put in several days on his engine, it'll be a long time before we're diving again."

The argument was a good one, for Berduk had a family to feed. Diving for sponges lasted only a season, and then they had to be satisfied with fish, which were much less profitable.

"Pity," Berduk said, as he went off. Turhan stayed where he was, looking at Stavros. He tried to persuade himself that he must dislike him, since by definition a Greek was unlikable, at least according to the theory cherished by Berduk and some others. But the resemblance disturbed him too much, as did the fact that the sleeping boy looked so vulnerable. The collar of his shirt had slipped open again, and Turhan fastened the top button with a brotherly hand. Then he stretched out on deck for the two-hour siesta before diving began again. In his turn, he sank into a deep sleep.

That evening, Stavros, revived for the second time, began to enjoy his adventure once more. Perfectly at ease, he pretended to know nothing about the working of a sailing vessel, and left the exhausted men to manipulate the halyards and the boom. The caique was coming in on a light headwind and they still had to tack several times.

Leaning on the rail, and resolutely turning his back on the temptation of the Greek islands filing past on the port side— Tilos, Nisiros and finally Kos—Stavros examined the indentations of the Turkish coast with the closest attention, behaving almost like a tourist. The voices around him did not disturb him, for he did not understand the remarks made at his expense. Nor did he do more than glance at Turhan when the boy came aboard from his dinghy. This was not his double, this Turk with his haggard face and blotched skin. He had nothing in common with Stavros, whose irrepressible youth was bubbling over, eager for the unexpected.

Bodrum: known to Stavros the Greek as Halicarnassus, native land of Herodotus, the Greek historian of the fifth century B.C.; and also of the King Mausolus, for whom in ancient days a sumptuous tomb had been erected, the Mausoleum, one of the Seven Wonders of the World. Stavros knew the history of every single one of the towns of Asia Minor which his ancestors had surrendered to the Turkish barbarians. He knew also that the Knights of Rhodes had, at the time of the Crusades, built a castle at Bodrum as imposing as the one in Rhodes itself.

The caique came into the little port just as the sun's last gleam was fading from the sky. He saw the formidable ramparts before him; and it was Stavros who came home, and the others who were the intruders.

Yet he was the one to be jostled as they disembarked, as Berduk invited him to land with a brutal shove. On the quay, it was the Turks who were yelling to each other, and the muezzin who, from the top of his minaret, invited the faithful to pray to Allah. Stavros was not in Halicarnassus, but in Bodrum. His sweeping glance took in the port and its houses, reddened by the setting sun, leaning against the hills. It was an enclosed world—a fact he knew because he had so often studied maps of the area—the ancient Caria, cut off from the rest of the country by a hostile mountain mass, difficult of access. There could be no better place for his enforced stay than this little town with its face turned to the sea, joined only by a corkscrew road to the next large village, about fifty miles away.

The island of Kos, Greek of course, lay opposite, at once a temptation and a source of hope whenever Stavros should feel homesick.

But would he suffer any feelings of this sort? The narrow paved alleys through which he walked behind Turhan, were lined with modest whitewashed houses that reminded him of certain quarters of Rhodes. The children playing on the doorsteps could easily have had names like Yannis or Nikos, Helena

or Melina. There were the same black eyes, the same neatly
braided pigtails on the girls, the same close-cropped heads on
the boys, that Greek children had. Stavros could not suppress
an instinctive movement of friendliness towards them. To avoid
any such involvement he concentrated all his attention on the
boy who plodded ahead of him wearily.

One following the other, they reached their goal. An alley,
like all the others. A white wall pierced by a narrow door.
There was a man by the door, holding his *seprah,* the Moslem
rosary with its ninety-nine beads, between his fingers. By his
side stood a hookah, its long tube wound round the container
filled with rose water. Beneath the peak of his cap, his eyes
were closed in prayer or meditation; or they were, perhaps,
sightless. When they opened, Stavros noticed that they did not
blink. Yet the two boys were so strikingly alike that no one
could have remained unmoved by their resemblance.

"You have someone with you today?" Ismet asked his son.

"Yes, father. A boy who . . . who has a face so like mine
that I can't understand it!" There was a kind of panic in his
voice. Surprised, the father gestured towards Stavros.

"Come a little nearer, you there."

Turhan pushed the Greek forward, and the father made
him stoop down. The *seprah* fell from the man's hands, which
examined the stranger's features, lingering a while on the lips
more fleshy than his son's, the nose a little longer, the brow
wider. The extraordinary sensitiveness of his fingers noted dif-
ferences that were hard to see in the whole face, so strangely
like the face of Turhan.

"This boy is not so very much like you," the blind man
said at last.

"But, father, the others say . . ."

"Let them say."

Ismet turned towards Stavros.

"Say something, you there, so that I can hear your voice."

"He . . . he doesn't understand Turkish," murmured Turhan.

"Ah!"

The father's fingers crept to Stavros' neck, and discovered the gold chain hanging between flesh and cloth. His face showed a sudden displeasure.

"Do you know what you've brought to me? I should have guessed from his thick lips!"

"We found him on the shore, half drowned," said Turhan eagerly. "The others want to pass him off as my cousin, to have a bit of fun with him before letting him go."

"Your cousin!"

"But this boy is not my cousin, he's my guest, father. You understand!"

Ismet was about to protest, when three little girls bolted out of the corridor that led into the interior courtyard. All three were laughing, as graceful and lively as three young kittens.

"Turhan! Turhan!" they shrieked, as they flung themselves on their brother.

Then the eldest, not quite six years old, stopped short, her finger in her mouth. Puzzled, she stared at the two boys.

"There are two Turhans today," she concluded, and she dragged her sisters to make a circle round Stavros' legs, as they burst out laughing again.

"Zehra! Yildiz! Aissa! Leave Turhan in peace! You know quite well that he is tired when he comes home!"

The voice belonged to a young girl of about fifteen, who stopped speaking as she halted on the threshold, staring at Stavros, her eyes wide with surprise.

"Leyla!" That was the harsh voice of the father. "Go in at once, do you hear?"

Since his alert ear heard no sound of footsteps on the beaten earth of the corridor, he said again sharply, "Leyla!"

This time the young girl withdrew, her curiosity unsatisfied.

"You children, you go in as well," the blind man added.

"Oh why? Why?" they chorused, as they obeyed.

Ismet turned to his son.

"Do you really intend to introduce this Greek into our household?" He spoke sternly.

"No one must know he is Greek," Turhan said quietly, looking around to make sure that no indiscreet ear had overheard his father's words. "That's agreed with the others."

"That doesn't alter the fact that he is Greek. You are aware of it, and yet you've dared to bring him here and show him the unveiled face of your sister!"

"Father, it's been a long time now since any woman of Bodrum veiled her face before a stranger; you know that as well as I do. Those old customs are finished and done with."

"I won't have a Greek here!" Ismet cut the discussion short. Turhan made no reply. It seemed that with the loss of his sight, his father had fallen back into the darkness of old times, the time before the reform, before Ataturk. He had withdrawn from daily life, returning to the beliefs of his ancestors, dividing his time between his rosary and his hookah. When he was still working as a diver, his mind had been open to modern trends. Now his son was torn between the past and the future, his father's beliefs and the natural aspirations of his youth: and Turhan was too exhausted to rebel.

"Wait for me," he said now to Stavros, gesturing to him not to enter the corridor. He returned a moment later with a blanket, a hunk of bread, and a jar full of water.

"Come," he said this time.

Stavros followed him. He had not made the slightest movement throughout the discussion, not even to return the hugs of the children. He wanted now to take stock of his position. Up to this point he had thought of Turhan only as a Turk, a foreigner. Now, suddenly, Turhan had a particular identity: he was the oldest son of a family, and, so far as Stavros could see, the only bread-winner. He had sisters, a swarm of sisters, a tyrannical blind father, and he practiced a hard trade. He was no longer just a Turk, he was Turhan, a boy who must be considered with eyes unclouded by racial antipathy.

They had reached the western limits of the town, and now Turhan was setting out through the undergrowth covering the hillside. Stavros followed with some difficulty, his bare feet stung by thousands of nettles. Turhan continued to bear left, leaving the hovels of the suburbs behind. He finally came to a halt near the crumbling remains of a high wall.

"This is Greek," he said, placing his hand on the stones still warm from the sun. He put the blanket, the bread, and the water-jar down. Stavros understood. This was to be his home. A Greek among the Greeks, or at least where some vestiges remained of their passing over these hills. He wondered whether the choice had been dictated by kindness or contempt, but that was not important. He already liked his new home. His hands stroked the ancient stones; he smiled as he looked at his provisions. Bread and water, fit for a prisoner.

A prisoner? If anyone had ever felt free, he did at that moment, with Bodrum at his feet, and the sea and the sky for bedfellows. Just for a second, the idea that Turhan had brought him there to give him a chance to escape crossed Stavros' mind. The Turk was standing in front of him, no trace of hostility in his eyes, and suddenly Stavros wanted to sound his feelings. He pointed to the island that lay across the horizon.

"Is that Kos?" he asked. "Greek territory?"

Turhan's face remained impassive. Only his eyes showed the same anxiety he had felt that morning, when he had discovered their extraordinary resemblance.

Stavros, discouraged, shrugged his shoulders. It would be impossible to communicate with this boy, unless he made a great effort. He sat down, his back against the wall, and gnawed his bread hungrily. God! He was starving!

Turhan looked at him for a while in silence, then turned to face the setting sun.

"Yes," he said. "That's Kos. Kos, a Greek island." He looked at Stavros as though he wanted to say something of great importance: but he did not know a single word of Greek, so he had to give up. A moment later, he was swinging down the hill. He did not once turn to look back.

4

MERAL

Bodrum turned its back to the dawn breaking behind the rampart of its hills. The early morning sun streamed over the waves and the open sea, then came to waken the white walls of the town, before dipping slowly along the slopes covered with scrub. When it reached the boy curled up at the foot of the ancient wall, it set off fireworks beneath his closed lids. Stavros pushed the blanket away with one hand, and with the other rubbed his eyes to free them from the troublesome light. He sighed, flung his arms wide, met stones and sat up, utterly lost. He had forgotten everything about his escapade in a strange land.

Awareness returned at sight of the sparkling sea, and he found himself looking forward to the day just starting. He stretched himself, then drank water from the jar. There was just enough left to wash his face. His hands, rubbing his cheeks spattered with water, rasped over the hair of his new black beard, sprouting thick after two days of freedom. He needed a shave before he set out to confront the town. He would feel ashamed if he went there looking like a tramp.

He looked around him uncertainly. The sun flashed on a bottle at the other end of the wall. Providence must be on his side. He went over to the bottle, broke it against a stone, chose a long fine splinter like a blade and began blindly to shave off the unwanted beard. He worked carefully, unwilling to show a face striped with razor cuts to the enemy. For there was no doubt he was about to confront an enemy; he had no illusions about that. He knew that no Turk, whether he were called Berduk, Husseyin, Kacim or even Turhan, would allow a Greek to walk freely in the town, and keep quiet about his nationality, without very good reason: he had no hope that the Turks' intentions were friendly towards him.

He wondered what day it was. The day before yesterday had been Monday; today therefore must be Wednesday. He felt that if any harm had been intended, it would have happened the day before.

Tuesday had been considered an unlucky day by the Greeks ever since that Tuesday, May 29, 1453, when the Turks took Constantinople by assault. That had been the beginning, so far as the Greek nation was concerned, of an enemy occupation four hundred years long, a yoke they had been able to cast off only in the middle of the last century. Massacre at Constantinople, massacres during the War of Independence, massacre of the Greeks in Smyrna in 1922 . . . and more recently still in Cyprus, where Greek and Turkish communities had engaged in bloody guerrilla fighting.

Stravros shrugged his shoulders, as though he were shaking off the burden of both the past and his own future, which seemed threatening when linked with the huge and brutal form of Berduk.

He descended the hill with lively step, determined to keep his mind away from old history as he was determined to ignore the burning of his feet torn by the undergrowth. He came to a square shaded by tousled eucalyptus trees and clicking coconut palms.

"Why! Turhan! What are you doing here at this hour?"

"Hi, Turhan! No diving today?"

Stravros, unruffled, waved a hand in greeting to the men who had, naturally, taken him for Turhan. Word had not yet gone around about the other boy who looked so much like him.

The town was already wide awake, in spite of the early morning hour. It had to make up for the long siesta taken in the overwhelming heat of the afternoon. There were inns around the square, and from their doors, wide open on this sunny morning, came the savory smell of stew in which Stavros recognized mutton, peppers and eggplant. His stomach contracted in a sudden spasm, for the bread of the evening before was now a distant memory. It did not occur to him to be surprised at finding such familiar cooking smells in this place, any more than he was at first struck by the nasal twang of a melancholy song coming from a radio turned up too loud across the square. It was only when he came near to its source that he was surprised to discover that he could not understand the words. The melody could have been that of any popular Greek song, based as it was on the melodic scale he knew to be unfamiliar in Western Europe, and which he had believed to belong to his own country. However, in four centuries of occupation the Turks must have had ample time to copy Greek music and steal cookery recipes—unless it was not the Greeks who . . . He found that thought as infuriating as the whine of a mosquito, so he dismissed it from his mind.

He branched off into a street where the shops opened straight on to the narrow roadway. There, at least, the smells were more mixed: that of stale fish mingled with the sweet perfume of cologne.

Like a tourist with a regular passport, Stavros loitered in front of the shop windows. The street was given over to barbers' booths, selling shellfish as a sideline. Stavros had to peer through a veil of fishing nets in which spindles, conch shells, pearly earshells and spiny murex were imprisoned, in order to get a glimpse of the threadbare barber's chair: and where he expected to see jars of lotion, there was instead a notice offering gorgonia lace * or branches of coral for sale.

Stravros passed his hand over his chin, where he had been unable to avoid cutting himself. "Maybe you can pay here with a shell or a starfish," he thought to himself. "I must try it." He was contemplating a long tranquil holiday in this little port, forgetting for the time being that he had to make sure of his survival.

In one of the shops he came upon an antique amphora, its sides speckled with sea-parasites. Stravros frowned; this was altogether too much. He might be willing to admit that the Turks had a right to occupy this land that had once belonged to his ancestors, but that didn't mean he condoned their pillaging the wrecks that lay at the bottom of the sea. That antique amphora probably had no more value in the eyes of the barber who put it on show in his window than if it had been a shellfish.

"Hi, Turhan!" the children shouted, as they rushed down the street. Stravros looked after them, filled with fury.

"I'm not Turhan," he wanted to shout back. "I'm Stavros, I'm Greek, and this amphora belongs to me. It has nothing to do with you! You don't even know how to appreciate it!"

He discovered that although it felt fine to be full of goodwill, to take pride in sweeping away preconceived ideas, there were nevertheless certain things that could not be tolerated. Nor was his temper improved when he came out on a small triangular space that gave a view of the sea and the Knights' Castle.

"Turhan! You're very stuck-up today!"

It was a feminine voice, which was fortunate for its owner, because otherwise Stavros would have exploded, and shouted out the truth, simply for the pleasure of hearing Greek

---

* Gorgonia or sea-fan, a kind of polyp.

words reverberate against the walls. Compelled to be courteous, however, he made a vague gesture of greeting, but this time he could not get away with it so easily. The voice belonged to a young girl with a lively face beneath her nurse's cap, and inquisitive dark eyes that did not look as if she would be easily taken in.

"Now then, what's up? Annoyed? May one know why?" Meral had come up to him.

"Oh!—I beg your pardon!" she said, and her face reddened a little. It had been easy to make the mistake while she was a few yards away, but not once she drew near. That nose, that forehead, did not belong to Turhan. She made a swift recovery.

"Do forgive me," she said. "Are you by any chance related to Turhan?"

Stavros, of course, could not understand a single word Meral had spoken, but he suddenly thought that perhaps a nurse would have some knowledge of English. The possibility was enough to bring back his good humor, for he was talkative by nature and had suffered from his enforced silence the day before.

"Do you speak English?" he asked. Yes, Meral spoke English fluently, so he told her that he was a stranger, as he had already demonstrated by not understanding her native tongue. Then, because she was so different from the image he had made for himself of Turkish girls, he went on to explain how Turhan had found him and brought him to Bodrum.

A man was watching them from his doorstep. Meral led Stavros aside to a deserted old bridge thrown across a small inlet of the sea, on which fishing nets were drying in the sun.

"In other words," she said, "you're a bit lost here."

Stavros smiled, and the troublesome resemblance disappeared.

"You're Greek, aren't you?" she added.

"But don't you think I'm related to Turhan? Look at my face!" Stavros tried to make a joke of it, but when he looked at Meral's open face, he added hurriedly, "Yes, I am Greek. How did you guess?"

"The way you rolled the r in Turhan. I've met Greek tourists at Izmir, where I did my nurse's training. And what other kind of stranger could the sea bring here on a stormy day? Your islands are all along the coast! Do the police know? Are they going to send you home soon?"

"I'm here incognito!"

"Oh, that's daring! Our police are good, you know."

"I hope you don't think you should inform them . . . the men who brought me here didn't seem to want to. I suppose they find it amusing to see how I'll get by without papers or money. That suits me—I'd like to live here a while. But I'm afraid that being Greek means it won't be easy to earn any money. I don't want to be a burden to Turhan; he's got enough to do to cope with his family."

Meral seemed to be impressed by what he said, for without hesitation, she blurted out, "When you get hungry, come to the town hall. There's a center for social assistance. You'll find me there, and I'll give you some of the soup I make for the poor." She moved away as she spoke, cutting short a conversation that had lasted too long, as she was well aware. Stavros was forced to shout after her, in English,

"How can I find the Town Hall?"

"Ask for the Halkevi. Anyone will tell you where it is."

Stavros remained on the bridge, wondering whether to take advantage of Meral's offer, his pride offended by the necessity of seeking help.

"Hi! What are you doing here? I've been looking everywhere for you!" Turhan came up, breathless from his search up the hill and all over the town. He had begun to believe that the Greek boy had escaped. Everyone said that the Greeks could fend for themselves, and maybe this one had used his likeness to Turhan to deceive one of the fishermen. He must be a good swimmer, to judge by his exploit on the night of the storm, and Kos was not so very far from the headland.

Turhan hadn't yet made up his mind as to whether he would be glad or sorry if the Greek boy had got away. If Stavros escaped, Turhan would be left to face Berduk's fury, and that was no small hazard. Yet he wondered what would happen if Stavros stayed with them, and what sort of dirty tricks Berduk and Husseyin would plot against him. He guessed that the Greek boy must be anxious to get back to Rhodes. And yet here he was, lounging about on the bridge, just as if he were on holiday. So much the worse for him.

"Come with me," Turhan said.

Walking one behind the other, they came to the extreme eastern side of the town, where piles of sponges were rotting in the sun, a sickening stench rising from them. Berduk and Husseyin were already there. They had chosen a position up-wind to avoid the stink.

Stavros made a face. The morning had begun too well; now he would soon know what was expected of him. He would have preferred to meet Kacim rather than these two, who were beneath contempt. Even Turhan, with his obvious integrity, could do nothing to help him against them.

"The Sultan and his Grand Vizier," he thought. "Polyphemus, the one they call Berduk, seems to be in command, but in fact it's the other one, the one who wears his cap back to front and never says anything, who pulls the strings." He walked forward stoically: he had decided to accept their challenge, so now he must get on with it.

Berduk welcomed him with a bellow of laughter, his delight in having the Greek at his mercy far greater than his annoyance at having had to wait for him.

"Here comes the bear!" he said. "Now we can make him

dance!" He gave Stavros a shove that brought him level with
the stinking pile of sponges. Nearby was a shallow tank filled
with water, in which the decomposed sponges were soaking.
Stavros needed no instructions, for there were sponge-divers in
Rhodes as well. He knew that once the sponges were rotted,
they had to be trodden, squeezed, and pressed in order to get
rid of the black teguments and smell of chlorine, a repulsive
job if ever there was one.

"Well, what are you waiting for!" said Berduk.

Stavros rolled up the legs of his trousers and stepped resolutely into the water. It was one way of earning a living, after
all.

The three Turks went off to sit under a eucalyptus tree
and share a meal of bread, red peppers and tomatoes. In spite
of the nauseating stench of the sponges, Stavros found his hollow stomach clamoring for food. But he could expect no wages
until he had earned them, and so he went on treading.

"That's fine, lad! You've got a natural gift for it!" said
Berduk.

"Allah gave him feet so that he might use them," Husseyin
growled, and this statement unleashed Berduk's mirth.

"Did you hear?" he shouted across to Stavros. "We'll make
you dance as long as you have feet!"

Turhan said nothing. He was there against his will. Stavros was his guest, and he'd hated having to hand him over to
Berduk. But he did not know what else to do. Kacim had said
that it would take him four or five days to overhaul the engine
completely, for he had had to order new parts from Izmir, and
during that time the men would be out of work.

Turhan got up as soon as he had finished eating.

"I'm going to help him," he said.

"Are you mad?" said Berduk, forcing him to sit down
again.

"He won't get through it alone."

"Whatever he can't do today, he can do tomorrow." Normally this was work done by the wives of the fishermen, for it was unpaid. The men received a percentage of the sales value of the sponges ready for market. It was this fact which gave a special edge to the enjoyment of the Turks, as they watched a Greek doing women's work, which, in their eyes, and particularly in those of Husseyin, who was steeped in the teachings of the Koran, dishonored a man.

It was a long morning for Stavros. Limestone grit and grains of sand worked into the cuts on his feet. The sun, which at first only reached him through the topmost branches of the eucalyptus, soon burnt directly on his head, while it quickened the decomposition of the nearby pile of sponges, and drew an unbearable stench from the tank.

The boy's face was running with sweat. His shirt was sticking to his back, and he felt as though he were dancing on millions of pins. The sea was only a couple of yards away, a temptation he must resist. He had a fleeting vision of his uncle's garden in Rhodes with its flowering hibiscus and bougainvillea, the crisp tang of shrubs and the scent of roses, a vision that he had to push from his mind or he would not have had the courage to go on with his task.

The painful hours dragged slowly by.

"Let's tell him to stop for a while," Turhan suggested. Berduk, however, wouldn't hear of it. He wanted to force the Greek to beg for mercy.

"You trying to make me believe he's not as strong as a woman?" he growled.

"It takes four or five women to do what he's doing on his own," said Turhan. "And they work in the cool of the day and stop when they've had enough."

"Naturally, they do. They're only poor Turkish women. He's a Greek, so he must be a super-champion, judging by their conceit!"

Stavros did not pretend to be a champion, but he was determined to spoil Berduk's enjoyment. In spite of the heat, his
hunger and devouring thirst, and the intolerable burning of his
feet, he went doggedly on with his task. He was young and he
was going to show the Sultan and his Grand Vizier not that he
was as strong as any Turk, but that he was as long-suffering as
any Greek.

At noon the three others divided up a loaf and Berduk
took a share for Stavros.

"Here, catch!" he said, and threw it with deliberate clum-
siness, so that it fell into the tank. In silence, Stavros fished it
out, threw it to one side, and went on with his work as though
nothing had happened. But when the others stretched out in the
small amount of shade afforded by the tree to enjoy their siesta,
he stepped out of the tank, walked steadily down to the shore
on his sore feet, took off his shirt and plunged into the sea, the
cleansing sea.

When he felt refreshed, he returned to the eucalyptus, hung
his shirt on a low branch and stretched himself out beside the
others. Berduk watched him, completely taken aback, but there
was no trace of provocation in the Greek's manner, nothing
that could justify any violent outbreak. Berduk could only
snarl, "Can't you move further off? You stink!"

Turhan indicated an empty space beside himself, where
Stavros stretched out again and closed his eyes. The pulse at
the side of his neck throbbed; the cross on the end of its chain
bounced on his naked chest with the wild rhythm of his strong
heart; he was dizzy with hunger and thirst.

He became aware that something was being forced into
his hand. Turhan had saved a piece of bread for him. He
pushed it away. The ration he had earned was drying out on
the sand, impregnated with the smell of the sponges, and he
would not accept charity.

Stubbornly, Turhan proffered his water-jar. For a moment, Stavros pretended not to notice, but he could not hold out against this second temptation. He sat up. Berduk and Husseyin were asleep, their caps pulled down over their eyes to protect them from the sun. Turhan was looking at him with an enigmatic expression, and still offering the water. Then, his pride at last broken, Stavros gave in to the exhaustion of the morning's hard labor, and took the pitcher. He drank in great gulps, while the sweat pearled over his body.

When at last he put the pitcher down, he thought he saw a glint of triumph in Turhan's eyes, and felt a surge of anger. Turhan was going to pay for the fury that Stavros had held back all the morning. He had an overwhelming desire to hurt the young Turk, to make him suffer in full measure for his own exhaustion, his hunger and the burning agony of his feet, his loathsome work, the Greek amphora in the barber's shop, for everything, even including that date, May 29, 1453, that every Greek carries within him like a badly healed wound. His hands tightened on the water bottle in his effort to hold back his fury. There was a stone beside him. The earthenware jar made a dry sound as it broke and the water ran away swiftly into the sand. Berduk opened one sleepy eye, took in the scene, and postponed until later the task of thinking about it. Satisfied, Stavros stretched himself out once more and went to sleep as suddenly as though he had been knocked out with a hammer.

The evening was in some measure a small triumph for him. The pleasure the Turks took in baiting him lost its edge during those warm hours when they had nothing to drink. All three pretended to be unconcerned about the broken pitcher, and mulishly refused to go to fetch another, so now there were four of them suffering from thirst. It seemed to Stavros that he would be relieved of his penance somewhat earlier than had been intended. When the time came, he plunged into the sea again, as he had done at noon, and bathed for a long time. His head was spinning with hunger.

He went off alone, and none of the Turks attempted to hold him back or to follow him. The first person he asked directed him to the Halkevi, for he felt that now he could, without any embarrassment, accept a meal that he had well and truly earned. The Halkevi was a haven of coolness and cleanliness, and Meral was in charge. She was more than just a nurse, for she also supervised the several activities of the center. Stavros was not ashamed to let her witness his hunger and his exhaustion. At last admitting defeat, he flopped on to a bench and swallowed the broth she put before him without even tasting it.

Meral examined him closely, wondering what he had done with his day to be reduced to such a state. When he had finished his meal, she asked him about it, but his answer was evasive. The story concerned only himself. Himself and Turhan.

It was odd how Berduk and the other Turk, the taciturn one who opened his mouth only to praise Allah, had vanished from his mind, as though the adventure were simply a game to be played between Turhan and himself. He got up from the bench, to escape Meral's curiosity, and only just stopped a groan as he put his foot to the floor.

"Show that to me," she said, with authority, forcing him to sit down again. "Well, I must say, that's a nice sight! How far did you expect to get with your feet in that condition?"

"It's through walking barefoot in the brushwood on the hillside. My feet will harden. It will just take time." He made as if to get up again, but he had reckoned without Meral.

"Will you keep still?" she scolded. "I'm going to do something about this." She came back almost at once with a whole arsenal of creams, lotions, dressings and powders, as well as a pair of sandals, sandals that were simply soles with a ring to go around the big toe. Stavros gave in and allowed Meral to clean and dress the cuts.

"There!" she said when she had finished. "And I must insist that you wear your sandals when you go walking."

"No need to insist," said Stavros, laughing. "I didn't go barefoot for fun! . . . May I look around?" He gestured towards the rooms that opened off the corridors.

"Of course. Go ahead while I put all this away."

Men were playing backgammon in the next room. Some boys were arguing over a game of Ping-Pong, to the rhythm of music blaring from a radio. The room next to that was a library.

"I won't offer you any books," said Meral, who had come to join him, "since they're all in Turkish. But if you'd like to, you could come to watch a film tonight. The pictures speak for themselves."

Stavros smiled at Meral doing the honors of her house. It was quite clear that she wanted to prove to him that the Turks were not the barbarians the Greeks believed them to be. In another small room, girls were busy with embroidery and listening to records. Stavros thought he saw Leyla among them, but could not be certain.

The smell of ether came from another door.

"Here we look after patients who have only slight wounds, or the sick who need injections or dressings. Mothers bring their children here too, to be vaccinated."

There was no conceit in Meral's voice, but some pride in all that was being accomplished.

"Will you stay, then?" she asked Stavros when she had finished showing him everything.

"Will Turhan come here?"

"No. He doesn't come any more, now that he dives for sponges."

Meral's eyes darkened, for Stavros had touched a tender spot.

"In that case, I'll stay," he said.

He wanted to forget the Turkish boy for the moment, together with the proffered water, and the glint of triumph in
Turhan's eyes that might really have been a gleam of pleasure
at having brought comfort to another. Stavros knew with cer-
tainty that he had made too swift a judgment, and all that remained of his first day at Bodrum was the sharp prick of an uneasy conscience at the thought of the broken water-bottle.

5

BERDUK

The following morning, Stavros was already on the site when the three Turks came to the eucalyptus tree. He had thought a great deal about the attitude he would adopt, and had decided to behave as though his work were not just a rather cruel joke. So he would not refuse bread or break water-bottles, and he would forget that he was Greek so that the others might forget it, too. He would certainly never have thought of this if he had met only Berduk and Husseyin in Bodrum. But the town also sheltered girls like Meral and boys like Turhan, and for their sakes it was worth making an effort to show the Sultan and his Grand Vizier just how ridiculous they were.

The first thing to do was to share meals without waiting to be invited, for food was his due. So this second morning, when Berduk set out tomatoes, cheese, and a hunk of bread, Stavros took his share, but a modest share to show that the frugality of the Greeks equaled that of the Turks. After which, he went back to work, humming a tune that would have been perfectly acceptable to the local radio station.

Berduk and Husseyin couldn't make it out. The joke had lost its point. They had hoped that the Greek, sickened by his labor the day before, would have tried to run away, or at least to dodge the drudgery. And that would have been something to laugh over for a long time. Secretly, what they had really intended was to show Stavros up as a coward and a weakling.

The Greek disconcerted them, for they could not guess what he hoped to get out of it. He certainly could not find any pleasure in such loathsome work. That thought brought the beginnings of a stupid smile to Berduk's face, and to Husseyin's a cunning one, like that of a cat dreaming in the sun.

Turhan understood Stavros better. In his place, he would probably have behaved the same.

At noon, he took it upon himself to call Stavros, who made a gesture of thanks, and went off for a short bath before coming to sit beneath the eucalyptus. He was as hot as he'd been the day before, but much less exhausted. This time, he had not worked on an empty stomach, and the cuts on his feet were protected by the dressings Meral had put on. Of the four, Husseyin was undoubtedly the one who felt most ill at ease, for he disliked the idea of breaking bread with an infidel.

In the evening, Stavros returned to the Halkevi, this time as a visitor. He passed Leyla on the threshold.

"Wasn't that Turhan's sister who just left?" he asked Meral when he found her.

"Yes. She came for some books. Does that surprise you?"

"A little, yes. Her father seems to want to keep her away from all eyes." He told her about the scene on the evening of his arrival.

"I know." Meral was smiling. "But don't believe that young people submit blindly to parental authority of that kind. They still respect our old customs, but they are emancipating themselves as well. They all have a strong desire to educate themselves. Leyla doesn't go out much, but she studies at home, and soon I shall try to persuade her father to allow her to work with me."

"That won't be easy."

"More than you think. Ismet is one of the finest men I know, but too much withdrawn since he became blind, and that puts him at the mercy of the old beliefs."

"And of the old enmities," Stavros muttered. "He would not open his door to a Greek."

Meral shook her head.

"You're wrong there. He shut his door to the stranger, not to the Greek. When we found ourselves confined to the narrow borders of modern Turkey, we became a little like Ismet when he lost his sight: we became suspicious of everyone who came from outside. In the North we distrust the Russians, who find it hard to accept our control of the Black Sea at Istanbul. Here, we distrust the Greeks still more, because you are installed all along our coastline, like inquisitive neighbors always ready to watch everything we do through their windows!"

"The past . . ." Stavros began.

"We are looking towards the future," Meral said firmly.

"You may be, but not men like Berduk!"

"I don't know this Berduk very well."

"He's not exactly crazy about the Greeks, and I'm afraid that he certainly hasn't forgotten the past."

"He follows a hard trade, with no time to think, or to educate himself. His world revolves round a few accepted ideas. If one of them is a grudge against the Greeks . . ."

"Then I must put up with it," Stavros finished, scowling.

"No one's forcing you. Why are you staying here?"

"Out of curiosity. Whatever you may say, we don't see what you're doing from our windows opposite. Though we'd very much like to, I can assure you. We young ones hear all sorts of things about you and we'd like to be able to judge for ourselves!"

"And then you have to fall in with someone like this Berduk!" said Meral, crossly. "You'll take a very false impression of our country back to Rhodes."

"There are others besides Berduk. I know that type of man, we've several of the same kind at home. I won't base my opinion on him."

"You've a critical mind, and that's good. But Turhan hasn't. He's the sort of boy who'll follow anyone. It's a pity that this Berduk is his teammate. He deserved better than that."

"Couldn't he take up some other work?"

"When his father went blind, he had to cope as quickly as he could. The family had to eat. His father's job was going, so he took it, in spite of anything I said. He was too young for all that diving. The sponge beds are often thirty, forty, fifty feet down, and the divers have no apparatus."

"They should have modern equipment."

Meral smiled.

"There are not enough beds round here to justify a big commercial operation. Mustafa would never consider anything but the traditional way of diving with his own workers."

"Turhan could work for someone else."

"Sponges pay better than fish, though not much. And it's not as simple as that. We are by nature indifferent to the way we live. It's ten times more difficult for us to achieve progress than for any other race. Here, in the Halkevi, I fight as hard as I can against this deplorable apathy . . . but Turhan doesn't come to the Halkevi any more."

Meral, at least, had chosen not to remain indifferent. Evening after evening, Stavros sought her energetic and sympathetic company with renewed pleasure. He had asked her to send off a letter to his uncle, to assure him of Stavros' safety and to explain that Stavros intended to remain in Turkey for some time.

Browsing in the library, he had come across an English-Turkish dictionary, and had begun to learn lists of words, particularly those dealing with daily life and fishing. Like many Greeks, he had a gift for languages. Odd sentences and snatches of conversation, heard here and there, fell into place around the vocabulary he had acquired. For the next six days his life followed the same routine: the day was spent cleaning sponges, the evening at the Halkevi, and the night in peaceful slumber at the foot of the ancient wall.

During the same six days Berduk and Husseyin were constrained to watch Stavros treading the sponges, then shaking them until they were ready to put into an acid bath to remove the limestone particles from the tissue. Six days spent in total boredom beneath the euclyptus; yet they could not go off elsewhere without admitting their defeat. They had to pretend to enjoy the sight of Stavros dancing in the tank, and for the last few days Berduk was unable to simulate any sort of pleasure. He was consumed by a sullen anger against the Greek, who had refused to allow himself to be humiliated. He was tempted, just so that he could have the last word, to boast of the fear he had inspired in the Greek, who had not dared to falter in his work, but that satisfaction was denied him when Turhan asked, for the tenth time,

"Why does he stay? I don't understand why he's staying in Bodrum."

"You're such a perfect host," said Berduk, hiding his mortification with a guffaw of laughter.

It was Turhan who, on the sixth day, told Stavros that his penance was over. He had noticed that the Greek now knew some Turkish.

"Tomorrow, finished," he said. "Tomorrow, for us, diving. For you, a free day."

Stavros understood everything but the last word, whose meaning was easy to guess. He would not be at all sorry to leave the work, but there was the problem of food.

He was reluctant to seek Meral's advice. He sensed a certain reserve on her part whenever she was reminded of his irregular position in Bodrum. She was already worried about hiding the real identity of Turhan's so-called cousin, and to ask her help now would be to involve her still more. He might have to go away without knowing any more of Turhan than what Meral had told him.

Turhan, who was inaccessible. Turhan who rested while Stavros worked, and would now be working while Stavros rested. Turhan who, every evening, mysteriously disappeared.

Before returning to the town, Stavros always bathed in the sea, partly for pleasure, partly to get rid of the clinging stench of the sponges. When he came out of the sea, the three Turks had always gone. Turhan had never once waited for him, and he had been disappointed. He had looked for Turhan in the town and had even dared to ask for him at Ismet's house.

"Is Turhan here?" he asked in labored Turkish.

The blind man, who had recognized his footstep, growled an unfriendly "No," and when Stavros had persisted, "Where is he, please?" he had only shrugged his shoulders.

Stavros had looked everywhere for Turhan, except in the gloomy back rooms of the cafés. Yet that was where he was, with Berduk, Husseyin and the other fishermen. It was their custom, after the hard days spent in diving, to relax with their glasses, enjoying noisy discussions that went on endlessly around the same few subjects. There was little or no alcohol in the glasses. Some, like Husseyin, were forbidden it by their religion; and for others their job of diving made it dangerous, so most of them drank sweetish syrups, or *ayran,* made from whipped yoghurt. Berduk alone, with his herculean strength, allowed himself to drink *raki,* a liqueur made from aniseed.

The huge Turk badly needed the comfort and warmth of alcohol on this last evening before work began again. That damned Greek had held out to the very end, and with a smile on his face all the time. It was an insult, an insult to Berduk himself. He could not remember whether it was Husseyin or himself who had had the idea of making him tread the sponges

—certainly Husseyin's ideas were always bad, and Berduk's always good. Berduk kept scowling at his accomplice. Beside him, Turhan was twisting the stem of his glass and looking thoughtful. He did not expect to see Stavros again, for he felt sure the Greek would find some way of leaving tomorrow. Turhan felt sorry about it for obscure reasons. Perhaps he'd liked the boy he'd known for a few days only, or perhaps he admired the way the boy had adapted himself. For his part, Turhan found it extremely difficult to make any change in his habits; otherwise, he would be out walking round the town with the Greek, and not sitting here beside Berduk, bored to death.

A torrent of light music from the radio poured over them. Conversation at Berduk's table was about the fishing planned for the following day. They hoped that the crew from Fetiye had not discovered the sponge bed. Those splendid soft Syrian sponges were worth at least double the price of the ordinary ones. As it happened, Mustafa had never before taken his men to that particular spot. It might well be that it belonged in fact, if not in law, to the fishermen from Fetiye. But that was the one thing that no one was going to admit.

They grew heated over the argument, some maintaining the rights of the first-comers, others insisting that if they found another crew there, they'd have to give way. The music suddenly stopped. A solitary voice began to read the news of the day. There was a reference to incidents in Cyprus, which were of course attributed to the Greek community on the island.

At once the men fell upon their favorite subject: Cyprus, the island that had scarcely escaped from English dominion when it was torn apart by the struggle between the Greeks and the Turks who shared its territory. The misdeeds of the Turks were forgotten as the men accused the Greeks, in the same way that in Greek cafés all over the islands, at the same hour, the misdeeds of the Greeks were forgotten in accusations against the Turks.

A veteran (among the sponge divers, a man of thirty-five is a veteran) took the floor.

"You'd think they hadn't got any blood in their veins, the Turks over there! All the same, we've given those Greeks a good thrashing from time to time!"

From there they went on to recall Smyrna in 1922 and, of course, that distant May date of 1453, one of the dates that no Turk, even the most illiterate, ever forgets.

"I was in Istanbul in May 1953, when they celebrated the five hundredth anniversary of our entry into the town. You should have seen it! All the officials in full dress. Speeches, and then more speeches! And the gaiety in the streets! Some of the youngsters stormed the ramparts—not that there's much of them left!"

The man burst out laughing.

"Seems that while all this was going on, the Greek churches were tolling the passing bell!"

"And so they might," growled Berduk, swallowing his *raki*. "Stupid to meddle with us!"

"You're right there! From what they said, three days of sacking the city once it was taken. And sixty thousand Greeks led away to slavery."

"Plenty to blow trumpets and bang drums about," growled Berduk. "I wish I'd been there to see it!"

"It's all a long time ago now," Kacim said, conciliatory. He had come to join the others, now that the last touch had been put to his engine.

"A long time ago! And is Cyprus a long time ago, then?" It was Berduk who was shouting that, the veins on his forehead swelling. He beckoned the waiter to bring him another drink.

"Don't you think you've had enough?" Kacim suggested. "Have you forgotten that you're diving tomorrow?"

"So what? Do you think I'm soft, like these Greeks? Have you taken a good look at me?"

"All right, have it your own way," said Kacim. "I was only thinking of your own good!"

Berduk swallowed his drink in one gulp. "That's the sort of lad who'd defend the Greeks!" he shouted wildly.

Kacim shrugged his shoulders.

"I'm not defending them at all. I see things as they are. With them, it's the same as with us, there are good lads and bad ones."

"I'm telling you there aren't any good ones among them," howled Berduk, at the height of his fury. "I'd have liked to be there that day, beneath the walls of . . . of their Constantinople. You'd have seen something!"

He ordered another drink.

"Because if I'd seen any Greeks, I'd have shown you what I could do, then and there!"

"Calm down," said Kacim, putting a hand on his arm. "Calm down and stop drinking."

But Berduk shook him off with a rough gesture. He was growling like an animal, dwelling on his anger. Turhan was looking at him with terror in his eyes. His mind suddenly released, he found he could follow the obscure processes of the big man's thoughts; and he knew where his murderous desires would end. He wished he could stop himself from hearing anything more. But his senses were so sharpened that he caught the words the others missed when Berduk got up, sent his chair crashing, and growled, "I know at least one Greek, and he's going to pay for all the rest."

6

A DANGEROUS GAME

Turhan was running. He must warn Stavros quickly. He had left the café on Berduk's heels, and had seen him stagger drunkenly in the direction of the hills. Turhan wished he had never told Berduk that Stavros was sleeping in the open air, and wondered why he must always truthfully answer any question put to him, as if truth gushed spontaneously from his lips, like water from a spring.

He deliberately took the opposite direction, thinking that with luck he would find Stavros at the Halkevi. He had learned that the Greek boy spent his evenings there when a neighbor told him, "I saw your cousin there. He seems to like it."

Turhan ran. Night had fallen, and people were sitting by their doors, enjoying the cool air. Scented smoke rose from the hookahs the men were smoking on the pavements. It was an hour of tranquility. Yet one man had broken away into the hills with murder in his heart.

"Hey! Where are you off to so fast?" they cried after Turhan. "Have the sponges learned to swim? Are they making for the open sea?"

Turhan rushed into the Halkevi like a whirlwind and said

to the first person he met, "Have you seen my cousin here this evening?"

"Your cousin? There's a boy who looks like you in the library."

"That's him," said Turhan with relief. But when he came upon Stavros he didn't know what to say. He knew he must warn him. When Berduk discovered the empty nest up in the hill, at the foot of the old wall, he would come to look for Stavros in the town. It was only chance that he hadn't come here first. Turhan shuddered at the thought of the public outcry that would have followed, with its serious consequences for Stavros.

"What do you want?" said the Greek, fumbling for the words.

Turhan hesitated. He knew that, for once, he must disguise the truth. If Stavros were warned about Berduk's murderous fury, he would not run away from it. And Turhan could not explain how very great the danger was this time.

Suddenly, an idea came into his head. He said quickly, still out of breath, "I came to suggest a game."

Stavros frowned. He could not understand what Turhan was doing there.

"A game," Turhan repeated.

"A game?"

Stavros went to find the dictionary, gave it to Turhan, who feverishly turned the pages. At last he found the word, and pointed to it.

"A game!" said Stavros, astonished. It was the last thing he was expecting.

"Yes, a game. You will be Turhan. And I will be Stavros. Do you understand?"

Stavros smiled. Turhan must want to play a practical joke on someone.

"I'm Turhan," he said, to show that he would cooperate.

"You'll go and sleep in my house tonight. And I will go out to the hill."

Turhan mimed his words to make Stavros understand more easily.

"Me, in your house. You, on the hill. Yes," said Stavros. "I understand. But for your father I am Stavros, not Turhan."

The blind man would not be deceived for a moment, but Turhan swept that objection aside.

"You agree?" he urged.

"Agreed!" said Stavros.

And then Turhan smiled. That in itself was an event, for he found little to smile about normally. His smile gave his face an air of great goodwill, that moved Stavros. Maybe, after all, the Turk felt some remorse at having left him to sleep in the open, and wanted to give him the chance to spend the night in a bed.

"Give me your shirt," said Turhan.

He closed the door of the room to make sure they would not be disturbed, and took off the undershirt he was wearing. Stavros understood. He unbuttoned his shirt and handed it over.

"Give me your chain as well."

Turhan held out his hand for it, and Stavros frowned, feeling that the joke was going a little too far.

"Yes, you must," said Turhan.

Now that he came to think of it, Stavros realized that if anyone were suspicious it would be better if he did not find such an irrefutable proof of Stavros' identity on him. The game was developing well. He must take care not to say much, but Turhan was not exactly talkative, so it would not seem odd.

But before he assumed this necessary silence, there were certain questions Stavros wanted to ask: among them the reason why Turhan had waited until now to make his odd proposition and why such haste was necessary.

He turned aside to look at the dictionary again, when the sound of the door warned him. Turhan was rushing out, pushing the last folds of the shirt into the waistband of his trousers.

"Hey! Wait! What . . . ?"

Stavros' questions remained unanswered.

Turhan made his way out as rapidly as he had come in. He made a gesture of greeting to Meral, who watched him go by, wondering whether it was Stavros or Turhan. That was Turhan's way of moving, but Stavros' shirt. If it were Stavros, it was odd that he should slink out like a thief, without exchanging a word with her, when he was usually so talkative.

She watched him go out into the street and start running. A footstep made her turn around. Here was the other one now, the Greek—or the Turk. The clothes of the Turk, the walk of the Greek. He passed in front of her with the same gesture of greeting. It must be some game, and if so, she hoped it amused them. She had other things to do than guess riddles.

Turhan was running again. He had to reach the wall before Berduk, to do battle with his maniacal fury up on the hill, far from the eyes of the town. Luckily the huge Turk was not accustomed to country walks, particularly by moonlight. It would be difficult for him to find his way, but his anger would feed on each false step and every scratch from thorny scrub.

Turhan ran, his chest as tight as if he had dived sixty feet down. He heard an oath, then another. The enemy had not yet arrived. Turhan reached the wall, and sat down to get his breath back. Now he must put on the skin of the Greek, so that Berduk would be deceived, for if Berduk guessed what had happened he would become even more enraged.

Turhan decided that the Greek would not yet have gone to sleep at that hour. He would probably be looking out at the sparkling sea. He would hear Berduk coming; he would be on his guard, at first, and go to the other side of the wall. He would not run away, for a Greek does not run away from a Turk. There was nothing he would not rather do—like treading sponges with a smile on his lips, for example. Provocation.

Thus Turhan discovered that, disguised as Stavros, he was going to pay off old scores of his own against his team-mate, Berduk. He would stand up to him at last.

Now the sound of swearing was keeping pace with the rhythm of stones rolling under Berduk's feet. He sounded like a bear, a bear with all his claws intact and his muzzle sharpened.

"Where are you hiding, you dirty Greek," he shouted when he saw that he had stumbled against the wall.

"Here," said Turhan, in the same sing-song accent that belonged to Stavros.

A sort of roar answered him. Berduk had seen his shape silhouetted against the sky.

"Hiding behind the wall, of course. Coward! As if you didn't know that a wall never yet stopped a Turk! I'll show you!

"Coward!" he howled, to frighten the hated silhouette that made no movement of retreat.

Turhan said slowly, "What do you want?" separating the words as the Greek did.

Berduk roared with laughter.

"Come here, my pet. Come closer, so that I can tell you what I want. Come on now."

He had reached the other side of the wall, near enough for his breath to hit Turhan full in the face.

"What have I done to you?" Turhan said.

"What have you done? You're a Greek, and I sweep the Greeks out of my way!" His grandiloquent gesture made him lose his balance.

"I will go away tomorrow," said Turhan gently. "Leave me in peace tonight."

He still had not moved, although he was terrified. For

Turhan knew that Berduk was drunk; Turhan knew that Berduk was a champion wrestler of enormous strength. But he knew also that to refuse to give way an inch to the enemy was the sort of courage Stavros would show.

In this case, unfortunately, not to give way to the enemy was to show contempt for him: and Berduk had already had enough of being treated with contempt for the last six days. He brought his two hands down on Turhan, and swung him up against the wall.

"I've got you," he growled. "Be cocky now, if you dare!"

Perhaps if Turhan had stayed completely still, Berduk's fury would have been mollified by his delight in at last securing proof of the Greek's cowardice. But the boy's Turkish blood now asserted itself. Turhan fought back. He had practiced wrestling since childhood, like all the boys in the town, and now he forced his body into the ritual parries, the traditional attacks, all of which increased the fury of his adversary.

The fight was unequal. Very quickly Turhan was nothing but a limp body in the man's brutal hands. He was no longer a boy, he was a sponge drifting gently in the heavy waters, as Berduk let his body fall to the ground. A stone rolled down the hill, and Berduk turned round, his fury that had been nourished by violence now dispersed by the end of the fight. He rubbed his eyes to dispel the illusion conjured up by . . . by what? Alcohol? Anger? Darkness? For Stavros lay there at his feet, and a second Stavros had come to call him to account for it.

He sighed. His clouded mind had just remembered: it was Turhan, not the Greek, who had come. Berduk laughed and growled, "That finishes him off!" as he nudged his victim with his foot.

Then, because he felt a sort of unease at the sight of the boy who stood there in the moonlight, he staggered away talking loudly, justifying his behavior to the stones and the bushes on the hillside.

"Somebody had to do it. They all wanted to, but not one of them dared . . ." Then, thirty yards further on—"So what, then! Why did Turhan look at me like that? I haven't killed his cousin. Greeks have tough skins. And if you want proof of that, look how he got away from the sea the other night."

Then, since a vague anxiety was creeping into his mind as he thought of that inert shape at the foot of the wall, he added with unexpected modesty,

"I'm not stronger than the sea, when all's said and done. I'm strong, yes. No one stronger in the whole of Bodrum. But the sea's something else. Can't tell me I've done better than the sea!"

7

THE
SECRET
LINK

Stavros had at first believed, when he caught sight of Berduk, that the man was there on the hillside in collusion with Turhan. He thought that Berduk knew about the hoax, had come there by arrangement, and that the struggle was simply part of the game. It was only when Turhan fell limply to the ground that he realized the wrestling bout had been a serious one.

He couldn't understand it. He wondered whether Turhan had suggested changing places so that he could settle a long-standing quarrel without interruption. In that case, why had he chosen this exact spot?

He suddenly realized. Berduk had come to thrash Stavros, not Turhan. Turhan had known his intention, and had deliberately chosen to take Stavros' place.

That thought spurred Stavros into action. He ran towards Turhan, and leaned over him. It was difficult in the faint moonlight to take stock of all his wounds. Turhan's face was bleeding. He was torn about the neck, where his shirt hung wide open. Berduk had snatched at the gold chain, which had bitten into the flesh before it broke. Yet these were perhaps the less serious injuries. With careful hands, Stavros went over Turhan's body, straightened his limbs cautiously, put his arm back into a normal position. Nothing seemed to be broken, unless his skull were fractured.

He slipped his folded blanket under the nape of Turhan's neck. Questions crowded into his mind, but he put them aside. He was overwhelmed with different emotions—pity, indignation, anger—but for the moment he must control them. It was time for action.

He went to fetch the water-jar he kept hidden in a hole, under a stone, while he was away in the daytime. The heat had not managed to evaporate all the water. He moistened his handkerchief and cleaned Turhan's face with infinite care. He discovered his split lip, swollen eye, bruised cheek. The water was cool. He dabbed Turhan's forehead and temples and tried to pour a little into his half-opened mouth, but the water spilled over his chin and ran on to his chest.

As Turhan continued to show no sign of life, Stavros was suddenly seized by an upsurge of fear. He had a moment of sheer panic, and then he remembered Meral. Meral would know what to do, and whom to inform.

He ran straight to the Halkevi, achieving the same feat that Turhan had done on his behalf a little while before in the opposite direction. He flung himself against the closed door, knocked, looked for a bell that did not exist, tried desperately to get in.

"It's closed at this hour," said a man who was enjoying the cool air on the step of a neighboring door.

"No cinema?" asked Stavros.

"Not tonight, no."

"Where does Meral live?"

The emergency had summoned all his knowledge of the Turkish language to his aid, but he did not know enough to understand the man's explanation. All he could discover was the general direction pointed out to him, the same direction as the quarter in which Turhan lived.

"Meral must live quite near him," he thought as he ran up the streets. "She seems to know the family well."

The blind man was at his post in his shabby chair. He grumbled to himself as he heard Stavros' steps go by. A little further on, a woman was scolding some children.

"Excuse me," said Stavros. "Where does Meral, of the Halkevi, live?"

"Over there, that door."

He hurried forward, and knocked. There was no reply. He knocked again, calling, "Meral!"

"Meral's gone to Mehemet's place, to give his little daughter an injection," said a man passing by.

Stavros did not understand a word of this.

"When will she come?" he asked. "When?"

The man shrugged his shoulders and went on his way. Stavros ran after him.

"A doctor. Where does the doctor live?" he asked.

The man started to give complicated instructions, all of which were totally incomprehensible to Stavros. Obviously the only thing to do was to wait for Meral, and hope that she would not be long, but he suddenly broke out into a cold sweat, thinking that Berduk might have gone back to Turhan to beat him up again. In a moment of panic he rushed headlong down the street, and bumped with great violence into a woman coming the opposite way. It was Meral.

"What are you doing here?" she said. "Where are you rushing off to?"

"I was looking for you. Turhan is hurt. You must come, quickly. He's unconscious and I couldn't bring him round."

"What happened to him?"

"A brawl," said Stavros curtly.

"With you?"

"No, I'll explain later."

"Where is he?"

"Up on the hillside."

"I've got my medical kit with me. Let's go."

"We must have a light. It's difficult to see anything up there."

"We'll call in at my place. I've got a storm-lantern."

Meral's voice was calm and very comforting. No words wasted, no haste either. Stavros grew impatient as she walked along at her usual pace, and turned the key in her door with a firm hand.

"Please hurry," he said.

"Is it so serious?"

"I'm afraid so."

"All the same, we'll take enough time to go through the higher part of the town," she said, as she came back carrying the storm-lantern. "We'll follow the path that goes outside the town. We don't want to attract attention."

"They'd take me for Turhan, in this darkness."

"They'd find it difficult to forgive me for taking a walk at night with a boy, even if it was with Turhan. I live a very independent life, you know. Too independent for a Turkish woman, so far as many people here are concerned. They still prefer to see a woman in the care of a father or a husband. As far as I can, I try to avoid shocking the feelings of my people. I must have their confidence if I'm to do any good here."

"Forgive me, I didn't understand. I was only thinking of Turhan."

"Suppose you tell me what happened?"

Stavros told her about the game, and the impersonation. "Obviously, I didn't have a chance of deceiving Ismet," he said. "He recognized me the moment I tried to cross the threshold of his house. Yet I'd tried to imitate his son's way of walking. I must be a rotten actor!"

"The senses of a blind person are extremely acute, you know."

"I'd imagined a thousand reasons for the game, and I thought Turhan would be disappointed with me. Disappointed, poor boy! All he wanted was to keep me away from the hill so that he could meet Berduk in my place!"

"It was Berduk who . . . ?"

"Yes."

"You saw him?"

"He'd just finished when I arrived. And I'm such an idiot that I watched him at it. I thought it was a game. I should have joined in and knocked him down. He went off when he saw me. And that's when I understood, when I saw Turhan fall. Let's go faster, Meral."

"We're already walking at a good pace. Don't be too worried. Turhan is a tough young man!"

"I'm afraid Berduk might come back."

"You think so?"

"It all depends on just how much he hates me. I'll leave you here and run on ahead."

"That would be pointless. Berduk has had more than enough time to finish off the job since you left the hill, if that was what he intended."

Meral was right, of course.

"I should have stayed with him," Stavros murmured.

"Of course not. You had to find help. You've done that, and all's well. So stop torturing yourself."

"It's easy for you to say!"

Then, because he was now obsessed by the question, Stavros asked, "Why has Berduk got such a grudge against me? I stayed in Bodrum because I was curious, not because I wanted to get even with him. He gave me a beastly job to do, and I did it. What did he want? For me to refuse? Or complain? Is that why? He wanted to humiliate me? Why? Because I'm Greek?"

"I think you're answering your own questions," Meral replied. "It is sometimes difficult to forget the past."

"But I'm not responsible for the past!" cried Stavros. "The past is over. And in any case, do you really think a man like Berduk bothers about history?"

"Maybe he does, if it seems to be repeating itself."

"How?"

"In Cyprus. If Berduk had been talking about Cyprus with his friends, that would have been enough to set him off."

"Yes, I see. Perhaps that's how Turhan knew what he was going to do."

There were other pressing questions, that were even more disturbing.

"Why did Turhan want to take my place? He never even spoke to me before this evening. He never once waited for me after work."

"We have a greater capacity for sacrificing ourselves than most other nations, you know. Turhan is very much a boy of his race. Look what he has made of his life: he's wasting his health and his future for the sake of his family, and he's never even questioned the need for it. What he's doing is just natural, as far as he's concerned."

"But I'm not one of his family! He owed me nothing! He could just have warned me."

"Would that have been enough?"

"Well . . ." Stavros hesitated. "Well, I could at least have waited for Berduk and taken the beating myself."

"That's what Turhan thought. He must have weighed you up in these last few days."

That still didn't answer Stavros' question. In Turhan's place, he would have warned the victim, and then stayed beside him. Then there would have been two of them to wait for the attacker.

Turhan had not moved from the foot of the ancient wall, and Berduk had not returned to it. Meral quickly lit the storm-lantern, and put it on the wall above the wounded boy.

"He certainly made a job of it!" she said, opening her bag. "Will you hold his left arm?" she asked.

She made a tourniquet round it, rubbed the bend of his arm inside the elbow with a piece of cottonwool and stuck a hypodermic needle into the swollen vein.

"There," she said. "He'll soon come round now. Meanwhile I'll clean up his wounds."

There were superficial cuts and scratches, and a good many bruises. His face, swollen, discolored and scarred, was unrecognizable.

"It'll be a long time before anyone can mistake us for each other again," Stavros was thinking.

He blamed himself for feeling glad about it, since any such satisfaction was out of place in the circumstance. He realized that he had disliked seeing his double pursuing activities that were not controlled by his own brain. Twin brothers would most certainly have some secret link that allowed each to accept the likeness of the other. There was nothing like that between Turhan and himself. At least, there had been nothing until now. But in the future . . .

When Turhan sighed and opened his eyes, Stavros felt an overwhelming sense of relief. He helped Meral to lift the injured boy and prop him up against the wall.

"The injection has done the trick," said Meral.

Turhan's uncertain glance rested on her. He lifted his hand to his face.

"Don't touch," said Meral, holding his arm.

"What . . . What are you doing here?" he said, shakily.

"Stavros came to find me."

Turhan turned his eyes to look at the Greek, and a brief smile flickered on his face. His scheme had worked.

Stavros did not understand. He wanted to know why Turhan smiled.

"Why did you take my place?" he asked.

In his eagerness he spoke in English, so Meral had to translate. Turhan looked slightly astonished.

"The Greek is my guest," he said, disarmingly.

Meral translated his answer. So that was the reason that had puzzled Stavros. Devotion to the family was taken for granted, and so was devotion to the guest. Turhan had not been able to offer him a roof, but he had at least made certain of Stavros' safety by risking the one thing he owned: his life. In Greece, hospitality is a tradition that goes back to the days of antiquity. Stavros was more than capable of judging the quality of the hospitality he had just been offered.

"Help me," said Meral. "I want him to drink a little."

Stavros held Turhan's head in his arms, while Meral lifted the water-jar. It was hard work, but the cold water revived the boy. He was in great haste to return home.

"Do you think he's fit to?" Stavros asked Meral.

"I think so, yes. It would be better. I'd like him to be examined by a doctor. His head was badly knocked against the stones, and there might be severe damage."

Stavros helped Turhan to stand upright. The boy staggered, then steadied himself. Stavros put Turhan's arm round his own neck to support him, and Meral went ahead to light the way.

All three plunged down the slope covered with scrub. The light of the lantern danced over the thorns and boulders ahead.

8

THE
CHAIN

At dawn the following day, Berduk awoke from a dreadful nightmare, paying for the excesses of the night before. As soon as he had reached the bottom of the hill, he had stopped at every café stationed along his route, drinking *raki* after *raki,* this one to help him forget his fear that he had struck too hard, that one to celebrate the success of his undertaking. Sometimes he looked at Stavros' gold chain with the pride he would have shown for a real trophy; at other times he could have wept when he felt it in his pocket. It was not that he felt any remorse, only that his mind was more or less turned upside down with alcohol.

Now came the dawn of a day to be spent fishing. Whatever happened, he must not delay. After all these days of enforced rest, Mustafa would be angry even if he were only a few minutes late. Berduk had already been threatened with being fired several times over, but he was a diver of exceptional endurance, and Mustafa had so far overlooked his wrongdoings, after swearing each time that he would not take him back. All the same, Berduk knew he must be careful not to wear out his patience.

Berduk had never before felt in such a shocking condition

at the beginning of a day's fishing; it was as though his body were as heavy as granite. He climbed aboard as clumsily as a landlubber, swearing wildly. Mustafa gave him a black look, and sighed.

"You can only find sponges on the seabed," he said to himself. "That great hulk will end his career sooner than he thinks."

Berduk flopped down, his back against the rail, indifferent to the handling of the ship. When the caique had rounded the castle of Saint Peter, Husseyin came to join his confederate.

"Kacim says you gave the Greek a good pasting," he murmured. "He saw you yesterday evening with his chain in your hand. He says he's going to inform against you if you've hit him too hard. He says you had no right to do it."

Berduk sniggered.

"I gave myself the right. You can't hit a Greek too hard. All I hope is that he's taken the hint and that he'll clear out before tonight, or else . . ."

A blaze of anger blurred his mind, still dulled by the heavy drinking of the night before.

"Or else, I'll do it again!"

"You'd better look out! If the police hear about it . . ."

"The police! You can be certain the Greek won't go to them! And as for Kacim . . ."

Husseyin raised his eyebrows. Berduk surely wasn't thinking of assaulting Kacim as well. He, who had never touched a drop of alcohol in his life, could not guess what was going on in Berduk's head.

"Does Turhan know?" he asked.

"He saw me last night just as I was leaving the Greek." Berduk shrugged his shoulders and went on, "Anyway, he did nothing to stop me yesterday, so he must be on my side."

This thought left him indifferent to the criticism the others might make. The huge Turk had a paternal affection for his young team-mate, even though he was incapable of expressing it except through unreasonable demands and even insults.

For the time being reassured, he stretched out on the deck and fell into a deep sleep. It was Husseyin who dragged him from it, an hour later.

"Hey! Turhan's already lowered the dinghy!" he shouted. "Better get going, pal. May Allah watch over you!"

Berduk sat up and rubbed his head, in which the wind seemed to roar as if a storm were brewing.

"Ooooh!" he moaned as he stretched himself.

"Shape up," said Husseyin. "Mustafa's got his eye on you. He suspects something."

Berduk got up, climbed over the rail and slid down the ropes hanging against the hull. As soon as he was in the dinghy, he splashed his face with sea water.

"Ah, that's better," he said.

He shook himself like a dog, and began to laugh.

"Allah does watch over me. Husseyin was right there. All I needed was an hour's sleep. Now I'm fine again."

Noticing that Turhan went on rowing in silence, his head down, Berduk added,

"What's up? You don't look too happy. But you only took an *ayran* yesterday evening."

Suddenly he shouted, "Hey! Where are you going? We've come far enough. Stop, fathead! Are you going to stop or not? You're still asleep, I swear!"

Still grumbling, he seized the oars to stop the impetus of the boat.

"If you've got so much energy to waste," he said, "you can dive first."

He held the trident out to the boy, and put the heavy stone that would help the diver to get to the bottom quickly on to the rim of the dinghy.

Turhan took the stone, and went down with it into the cold water. Berduk yawned noisily.

"It's not my day," he complained. "I don't have any luck. It would happen when the sponges are deep down!"

Turhan's head broke the surface, sending ripples across the water.

"Already!" said Berduk. "Impossible! I haven't even had time to bring the stone up! And where's the sponge?"

Turhan, hanging on to the side of the dinghy with one hand, was holding his trident in the other, but there was nothing on its sharp prongs.

"Where's your sponge?" growled Berduk.

The boy made a gesture of impotence. He breathed deeply and dived again. Berduk watched him, frowning. This time, when his shape rose in the water, he bore a catch. But when he came out of the water, Berduk frowned again, for the sponge was small.

"What on earth . . . what's the matter with you this morning? I'm the one who was drinking last night, but you're the one with the hangover!"

Another dive by Turhan brought a larger sponge, but it had been clumsily speared and torn by the trident, so that its market value was doubtful. Then another dive yielded nothing, and another, and then there was once more a torn sponge. Each time, Berduk shouted his anger. The other divers were laughing and joking about it.

"What a noise from one man!"

"Good job, it's not a shoal of fishes. We'd've been chasing them as far as Gibraltar!"

"Perhaps you're too near the edge of the bed," Husseyin shouted across. "Turhan should have realized."

"Turhan? More silent than his sponges," Berduk replied. "Just as though he swallowed his tongue with his *ayran* yesterday evening."

It was at this moment that the boy hoisted himself aboard, before he had finished his diving time. He even refused his team-mate's help. He sank on to the thwart, his face in his hands, his chest heaving.

"What's up then? Don't you feel too good this morning?" scolded Berduk, suddenly calm at this unaccustomed sight. "Try to rest, and I'll take my turn now."

His heavy bulk fell into the water, sending up showers of spray. Before he dived he said, "Hey! Don't forget the stone!"

When he resurfaced, he was abnormally out of breath. Turhan took the sponge from the end of the trident without saying a word. Disturbed by this silence, which he took to be a reproach, Berduk became engrossed in watching the little waves that lapped around his chest. Then he dived again, brought up a sponge, and then another. Each dive cost him a superhuman effort. He was fighting with the sea as he would wrestle with an opponent. The sea slipped over him like an oiled body, crushed his chest with its terrible weight, tried to suffocate him. He knew that those *rakis* were too much, even for his body.

It was all the Greek's fault.

He came up once more, his ears singing as if he were a beginner, and just as he surfaced he was seized with a fit of dizziness. He saw red before his eyes, reached for the side of the dinghy, failed to find it, and began to sink.

Then suddenly, there was air again, air that he could breathe in great gulps, relieving the heavy pressure. Turhan's hands were locked round his wrists, and he could see Turhan's face leaning towards his own. Gallant Turhan! Turhan eager to help his old friend Berduk! Turhan smiling! It was a fleeting smile, that made the boy look like the Greek. There was no way, it seemed, of forgetting the Greek.

Berduk pulled himself up into the dinghy. Turhan was looking like himself again. The big Turk passed his hand over his forehead. There was no doubt about it, he'd have to cut down his drinking. A splash in the water roused him from his discomfort. Turhan had dived again.

This time, he came back with a sponge as large as could be wished, skillfully speared by the trident, which had left only a tiny mark. That was the way to work. Berduk had always insisted that the trident was better than the knife, so long as you knew how to use it.

"Bravo, lad," he said.

Turhan was getting his breath back, but taking longer over it than usual.

"Well, what are you waiting for?"

Berduk was bullying again as soon as he had recovered his strength. He turned to the boy. Suddenly he noticed the thin white line round his sun-tanned neck, a line that could only have been made by a chain.

"I must be going mad," he said to himself, closing his eyes in an attempt to clear his sight. When he opened them, Turhan had dived again. He had found his normal rhythm now, staying down longer, and bringing a sponge back each time. The white line round his neck was still there.

"Why is that mark of a chain there? I never noticed it before," Berduk wondered. "That Greek's upsetting all my ideas. As if Turhan would wear a chain!"

It was certainly Turhan clinging to the boat, in spite of the mark on his neck. It could not be anyone else.

When it was his turn to dive, Berduk allowed himself to sink downwards with a sense of pleasure. At least there were no surprises down there; he knew exactly what to expect. But up above there was that ambiguous face, that smile he did not recognize and that thin white line round the neck.

At noon, on the deck of the caique, Berduk examined his team-mate closely while eating his bread. He found it impossible to decide whether it was Turhan or the other one, for he could only just distinguish them when they were together. Yet it was surely Turhan's exhausted and gloomy face he saw now. The Greek looked younger. In any case the Greek could not be on this boat. If he had any strength left this morning, he would certainly have used it to escape. With this thought, Berduk's confusion disappeared, and a smile spread over his face.

"Hey, Turhan, did you say goodbye to your cousin? He must have gone by now!"

The boy lifted his head and looked at him. A drop of blood hung from his nose, and he was wiping his mouth with a handkerchief stained with patches of red. Berduk's laughter stopped abruptly. Hemorrhages like that happened only to beginners, but Turhan was a long way from being a beginner. He must really be in a bad way to bleed like that. Torn between anxiety and a vague compassion, he growled, "Well then? Did you say goodbye? Yes or no?"

"No. Why should I?"

They were the first words Turhan had spoken that morning, and they were muffled by his handkerchief.

"Why should you? Why?" Berduk burst out, turning towards Husseyin. "Something tells me he won't want to stay any longer!"

Since Turhan looked coldly at him, and showed no sign of making a reply, Berduk, put out, turned once more to Husseyin for an explanation. Husseyin got up and drew Berduk to one side.

"That boy isn't Turhan," he said quietly.

"Not Turhan? Who is it then?"

"The Greek."

"The Greek!"

Berduk shouted with laughter. It was quite clear that Husseyin had not seen the Greek being soundly thrashed.

"I tell you it's the Greek," Husseyin repeated stubbornly.

"He's bleeding like a beginner, and he doesn't know how to dive. You said so yourself, at the top of your voice! You've spent the whole morning grousing about it!"

Berduk shrugged his shoulders.

"That doesn't mean much. I haven't been too good myself this morning. Does that make me Greek?"

Husseyin's obstinacy made him angry. He growled, "You think I was telling lies about the Greek? Well then—where else could I have got this, just tell me that!" He'd taken the gold chain from his pocket, and pushed it under Husseyin's nose.

"I don't know about that," said Husseyin, pigheaded. "It's still the Greek who was diving with you this morning. Perhaps you didn't knock him about as much as you thought you did."

"What about Turhan then? Where's Turhan? Why didn't he come fishing?"

"Only Allah knows," Husseyin murmured.

"Allah knows, I'll agree with you there," Berduk growled. "But I'll know too, you can be certain of that!"

He turned round and called with a voice like thunder, "Hey, Turhan! Come here!"

The boy got up, submissive, and came to join the two men at the stern.

"Do you recognize that?" asked Berduk.

He threw the chain to him, and the boy caught it in flight.

"Yes," he said.

His fingers examined the chain until he came to the link that had snapped. He took a knife from his pocket, opened the link with very great care, just enough to allow the next one to fit into it, and then he closed it with his teeth. He put his knife away, calmly fixed the chain round his neck and slid the cross beneath his undershirt.

"Thank you," he said with a smile. He turned on his heel, and went off to settle himself beside the coiled rope that the Greek had chosen the day of his rescue.

The caique was riding peacefully at anchor, rocking the men overcome by the heat. Gulls swooped in noisy circles in the sky. At the stern, Berduk, now totally confused, was complaining like a child.

"Am I going mad, Husseyin, or what? What's happening in here?" He struck his forehead with his fists.

"You should get some sleep. You'll feel better afterwards."

Husseyin made his companion stretch out on the deck.

"I know I half killed him last night, I know I did!" Berduk murmured before he slept.

Whatever Husseyin had said, the afternoon brought no solution to the problem. The boy—whether he was Stavros or Turhan—seemed to have been struck dumb and pretended not to hear the questions that his team-mate put to him.

"It is the Greek, then," Berduk said to himself. "He doesn't understand what I'm saying."

He eagerly examined the face that rose from the water, searching for traces of blows but finding none. The boy's skin was smooth, without the slightest abrasion.

"Yet he bled, last night," Berduk remembered. "I hit hard, and I had blood on my hands."

His face reflected his perplexity. The diver, whichever he was, took no notice of anything but the exhausting job he had to do.

"If it were the Greek," Berduk pondered, "he would be afraid. This one trusts me, so he must be Turhan."

The boy surfaced once more. The gold chain fitted round his neck in the exact position of the white line on the sunburned skin.

At the end of the afternoon, when Berduk took the oars to row to the caique, he put the question that had now become an obsession, "Tell me, you! Are you Turhan or are you the Greek?"

"I'm Turhan," the boy replied, with Stavros' smile.

Berduk's face was convulsed.

"Then take that off!" he shouted. He had let the oars go, and was pointing to the chain.

But the boy covered his throat with his hands, like a shield.

"No," he said.

That was his last word. After that, he was satisfied to listen to Berduk's bellowing with the same indifference that he would have shown to the howling of the wind in the sails or the misfiring of the engine: it did not concern him. It was for others to look out for squalls, or a breakdown, or this man's anger.

"It's the Greek all right," Berduk said to himself for the hundredth time that afternoon. "Turhan is afraid when I shout. He would not dare to disobey me. He would take that chain off."

Then the memory of Turhan intervening on behalf of the shipwrecked man, that morning after the storm, came into his mind; of Turhan, trying to make it easier for the Greek when he was treading the sponges. That must be the explanation. Turhan did not approve of Berduk's conduct, and so he was in rebellion. He had deliberately dived badly, and he had kept that cursed cross as a defiance.

Another fear crept into Berduk's heart. He wondered if, through beating up the Greek, he had lost Turhan's trust.

9
RAKI

Berduk's voice was almost pleading as he said to his companion, the moment he jumped on to the quay, "Coming to have a drink?"

The boy followed him without speaking. He was walking in exactly the same way Turhan walked when he was exhausted at the end of a day's diving in deep water, and the tired lines of his face made him look ten years older. Stavros—for of course it *was* Stavros—noticed this as he glanced at his reflection in a shop window. He had wanted to identify himself with Turhan, and he had succeeded beyond all hope. Sixty feet down, he had sloughed off everything that distinguished him from his double: his untouched youth, his arrogant vitality, his lively inquiring mind.

He sat heavily on the rough chair facing Berduk, whose wrestler's shoulders were bowed by his fatigue. He asked nothing more from life than to sit there for ever, existing like a vegetable, watered with sweetish liqueurs, his head nodding to the shrill music flooding from the radio. Meral's image came into his mind, troubling him for a moment. He remembered what she had said about Turhan: that he was indifferent, even apathetic, to the present conditions of his life.

"Meral ought to go diving, just for one day, and then she'd understand," he thought. "No one could persuade me to go to the Halkevi tonight."

He felt at home in the close atmosphere of this small, over-heated room. Nothing worried him: neither the plaster flaking from the walls, nor the raucous music, nor the dirt on the table. He felt attuned to Berduk, who was the only one other than himself to understand the weight of the sea that day.

His hand went to his ear, which had started to bleed again. This hemorrhage was a nuisance, yet easier to bear than the weight of stone he carried in his chest, or the fire that burned his eyes.

Berduk was looking at him.

"He knows that I'm not Turhan," Stavros thought. "He's known it all evening, and yet he's made no hostile move." He wished he could speak Turkish fluently, to be able to chat a little with the man, about simple things, for his mind was as exhausted as his body. They could talk about the quality of the sponges they had brought up or the misleading transparency of the green waters, and the shadow of the boat floating on the surface, more attractive than any star in a dark sky.

Berduk was looking at him, saying nothing. Apart from the two of them, the café was empty. He had brought the boy into a room not much used by the fishers, but Stavros did not realize that. Even if he had known, he would not have been worried, for he was no longer Stavros, but Turhan, a sponge diver, who was enjoying a well-earned rest after a hard day's work.

Berduk's glance lingered on the blood running from the boy's ear. The sea had been rough on him.

"You're in a bad way," he said. "Have a *raki*."

Stavros understood only the last word. He shook his head. "No," he said.

He had to dive again tomorrow, and he knew that alcohol was the worst enemy of the sponge fishers.

"Yes, you must," Berduk insisted, and without listening to any further protest, he ordered a glass of *raki;* one glass, not two, for he had chosen to remain sober. He had paid too great a price for yesterday's excess.

Stavros looked at the glass full of *raki.* It was tempting. He remembered having drunk a little alcohol at some family affair, and the cheerfulness that followed. Maybe the *raki* would relieve the weight on his chest, and the buzzing in his ears. He resisted for a moment longer, then his hand went out to the glass and he drank it straight off, without pausing for thought, just as he had dived for the first time, that same morning. A sudden heat flamed in his cheeks, but he felt no relief to his breathing or the buzzing in his ears. He pushed the glass away in disgust, and held his head in his hands, ashamed that exhaustion had robbed him of his willpower.

Opposite him, Berduk sniggered.

"Turhan never drinks *raki,*" he said as he got up. Stavros understood this time. He wondered if it were possible that the man had doubted his identity until that moment. If so, he might have to face again next day the danger he thought he had overcome so triumphantly during that afternoon. He was overcome with terror at the thought. Wild ideas of escape surged through his mind. Above all, he felt the need to seek courage in another glass of *raki.* He got up abruptly, determined to keep his self-control, and fell into step with Berduk.

Berduk went up the narrow streets with his heavy tread, greeting the people who greeted him.

"Good fishing today?" one of them asked, then another, then ten more, for that was the thing to ask of a diver returning home.

"Yes, good fishing," he answered with a smile, each time

turning to look at the boy beside him, for he was the best catch of the day.

Suddenly, Stavros understood where the man was making for. They were going to Turhan's home. For once, Ismet was not keeping watch beside his door.

"Anyone at home?" Berduk called out, and he walked in without waiting for a reply, dragging Stavros behind him.

Ismet was sitting in the main room. Under the yellowish light of an electric bulb, Meral was busy changing Turhan's dressings. The three little sisters were grouped around, watching with interest.

Berduk stood rooted to the spot. Here was the boy he had beaten up the night before, and what a fine piece of work it had turned out to be.

"Hello, Berduk," Turhan said, through the dressing over his split lip. "How's things?"

There was no trace of animosity in his voice. But Meral's withering glance so abashed the culprit that he said nothing.

"Is that you?" said the blind man. "It would appear that my lad here really has made a mess of things. Clumsy oaf! Fancy catching his foot in a rope and falling on the barb of an anchor. Poor footwork for a diver!"

"Yes, yes," stammered Berduk.

So that was the explanation Turhan had given his father. He still did not understand why it had been Turhan on the hillside last night. His eyes met those of Stavros, who was watching him. He wanted to cry out, "It's this one, not Turhan, who should have been hurt!" The whole situation was impossible. He felt ashamed, as though he had just beaten up Turhan in front of them all, Turhan, whom he loved like a son, and whom he had bullied only for his own good, to make him into an expert diver.

"You've someone with you," the blind man said. "Who is it?"

"Me," said Stavros.

"The Greek," the blind man said, half-rising.

"Meral!" Stavros spoke in English. "Will you tell Ismet that I have come only for news of Turhan?"

"Turhan! Turhan! There are two Turhans today!" the little sisters shouted, as they broke away from Turhan to cluster round Stavros' legs, as they had done before.

"This one isn't hurt," said Aissa.

"And he smells of sponges," said Zehra, stubbing her nose against his trouser leg. "You don't smell of sponges," she added, turning to her brother. "You smell of ointment."

"Did you try to go home?" Turhan asked Stavros. Meral translated into English.

"Tell him that I didn't," said Stavros. "I dived with Berduk and I'll go on doing so until he's fit again."

"But . . ." said Meral, taken aback.

"Tell him," Stavros insisted.

Meral did as he asked.

"He doesn't owe me anything," said Turhan, surprised. Stavros smiled.

"It's not a debt, but a game. Tell him that, Meral." Then he went up close to Turhan and said in a low voice, "Goodbye for the time being, Stavros. I'm Turhan, have you forgotten?"

He left the room without turning round.

"Where are you going?" said a small, clear voice. Yildiz had followed him, and now she took his hand. She had beautiful black eyes, and her two tight braids bobbed against her back as she walked.

"I'm going to sleep," said Stavros. "I'm tired."

"Why don't you stay here?"

"Sh!" He put his finger to his lips.

"Oh," said the little girl, with a knowing air, as though he had told her a secret.

At the door he passed a woman who, from her looks,

must be Turhan's mother. The sight of her brought back a blurred memory of his own mother, and reminded him of how much he missed her.

He dragged himself back to his place on the hillside, dropped down on his blanket, and lay there exhausted. Even the sound of footsteps in the brushwood brought no movement from him. He supposed it was Berduk coming back to make good his mistake, and he didn't give a damn. Even if the brute beat him up, Berduk couldn't make him feel worse than he did already. It wasn't Berduk, but a woman: Meral.

"Now we two will have it out," she said, crouching down beside him. "What idiocy are you up to? Are you so tired of living that you go diving with that Berduk, who wants you dead?"

Stavros turned over on his stomach, and had his face in his folded arms.

"Go away. You can't do anything for me."

"Oh yes, I can. I've brought you these tablets—they tone up the heart. Turhan told me the sponge bed you were working on is about sixty feet down. You'd never dived before, had you? I could see you'd had a hemorrhage. It's crazy to go at it bullheaded like that!"

"Don't need your pills," Stavros grunted, turning round again.

"But . . ." Meral began, then she leaned closer to the boy.

"You've been drinking *raki*. Are you mad? Anyone would believe you really did want to kill yourself! Drink *raki* when you intend to go diving again tomorrow?"

"Only one, Meral, only one glass of *raki* to give me courage."

"And did it?"

"No," Stavros admitted in a woeful voice. "I feel so awful, oh . . ." He wailed like a child.

"Sit up," said Meral, "and swallow this tablet."

Stavros, subdued, did as he was told.

"There," she said. "Now let's get to the point. Why did you take Turhan's place on the caique? For bravado? To needle Berduk? To show him that Greeks have plenty of courage? Or was it to help Turhan and his family? To pay back your debt to Turhan?" Meral's voice was stern, and she added, "None of these are worth risking your life for!"

"Berduk won't do me any harm now," said Stavros. "If he'd wanted to, he'd have done it already."

"I'm not only thinking of Berduk. I'm thinking of the harm you can do yourself by diving."

"Bah! The first day is always the most difficult. And now I've got your pills . . ."

There was a mocking lilt in Stavros' voice. Meral sighed with relief. Stavros was himself again.

"Why are you doing it?" she asked in a gentler tone.

"Turhan suggested a game. I'm playing it to the end."

"That's ridiculous. He saved you last night, and you want to pay your debt to him, I suppose?"

"No, I'm simply playing a game, I assure you. Since yesterday evening, I'm Turhan. And believe me, it's sometimes terrible to be Turhan. You should try diving. Then you'd know why Turhan doesn't come to the Halkevi any more!" His exhaustion showed in his voice, and the moonlight accentuated the weariness in his face.

"You must sleep now," Meral said. "If you really are going on with the diving tomorrow, it will be very hard for you."

"Do you think I'm not capable of going on with it?" Stavros grumbled.

"No. I just think it's an experience that shouldn't go on too long. If your game is to keep Turhan's job open for him, which is what I suspect, you can't win. Turhan will not be able to dive any more."

"He's seriously injured?"

"The doctor found a slight lesion in his lungs. He started to dive too young."

"Oh!" said Stavros. "I am truly sorry."

"You should be glad. If it hadn't been for that mistake last night, the lesion would most certainly have grown worse before Turhan went to see a doctor. Thanks to you, he's received his warning in time."

"Thanks to me! That's an odd way to look at things!"

"Don't worry! The only important thing is this: Turhan will do no more diving, and for your part, you've nothing more to do on Mustafa's boat."

"But I have," said Stavros very gently. "You're forgetting my family. I've a blind father, and four sisters, and a mother!"

"Do stop joking."

"I'm very serious."

"You're Greek. And it's not your family."

"Am I Greek? Truly? I heard about an illicit traveler who was Greek and burning with curiosity, but that's not me, Meral. That's no longer me."

"Be quiet and go to sleep. You'd be better off resting than talking all this nonsense!"

"I shall go to sleep because the nurse tells me to. Turhan is obedient . . . and he is so tired!"

Stavros stretched out full length with his face turned to the wall, and closed his eyes. Everything was spinning in his mind . . . Turhan, Berduk, Meral . . . what a lot of questions they kept on asking, all of them. But above all, Meral, who was as inquisitive as a Greek. She'd certainly found plenty of reasons for his actions, and they were all real. It was quite true that a mixture of recklessness, generosity and gratitude had led him to take Turhan's place in Berduk's dinghy. But that was not the whole of it.

Meral had not guessed the deepest reason. She could not have done so when Stavros himself did not know how to put it into words. He simply felt it stir somewhere in the unexplored recesses of his conscience.

Very near, a cricket chirped. Stavros' mind fastened on to it for a second, then sank into sleep. Meral, watching him, was torn between anger and sympathy. When she knew from his regular breathing that he was asleep, she strode down the hill, angrily wondering by what right this boy usurped the identity of a Turk. In this she was unjust, for she had forgotten that it was Turhan's idea in the first place, but she intensely disliked feeling obliged to a boy from the opposite shores.

She stopped abruptly. It was precisely thoughts of this kind that had brought Berduk to the point of lashing out blindly with his fists at a boy who had done nothing to him.

"I have no right to judge that man," she thought. "I'm no better than he is."

She went over the chain of events as objectively as she could, and was brought up short once more by Stavros' obstinacy over the sponge diving.

"Oh, let him dive, then!" she thought. "If it gives him so much pleasure! The important thing is that Turhan won't be diving!"

She thought for a few moments and then she smiled.

"If Stavros guarantees the maintenance of the family, Turhan might be able to educate himself so as to get a better job. He wasn't at all stupid before he committed himself to that confounded boat."

That was a comforting thought: so she could not understand why the realization of the many dangers that Stavros faced should overshadow her dreams of the future, like the cloud that had just drifted across the moon, and left the hillside in darkness.

10

DIVING

The following morning, Stavros wondered how he could have felt so wretched the evening before. His exhaustion had vanished after a good night's sleep. He looked at Meral's tablets with some uncertainty and wondered if he really needed to take them. Life was full of promise again. Then the memory of the *raki* he had drunk slipped into his mind, and he felt it would be a good thing to arm himself against further temptation. Overcoming his scruples, he swallowed one of the tablets in a little water.

Berduk was waiting resolutely for him on the quay, his heavy bulk barring the way to the caique.

"Good morning!" Stavros greeted him like an old friend. "Let me pass, will you?"

The familiar phrases came into his mind, fresh from a night's sleep, directly in Turkish. "Let me pass," he repeated, as Berduk stayed where he was.

"Get the hell out of here!" The man spoke between his teeth. Two policemen passed on the quay. Stavros glanced at them briefly.

"Who will you fish with if I go away?" he murmured.

"Hey, you two!" Kacim shouted from the caique. "Why don't you move?"

"We're coming," said Stavros.

Now Berduk was shuffling from one foot to the other, not knowing what to do. The presence of the policemen disturbed him, for the last thing he wanted was their help. He would have to put off his quarrel to some other time. He moved aside to let Stavros pass, but could not resist giving him a shove, which nearly sent him into the harbor.

"Hey!" Stavros said. "There are no sponges here!" He decided, as he leaped on board, to ignore Berduk's hostility.

"Hello, cousin, how are you?" said Mustafa. "I didn't even notice it was you; yesterday I took you for Turhan."

News travels fast in small villages. Everyone on board knew now that Turhan had injured his face, and that his cousin had taken his place on the caique. No one really believed Turhan's story of his accident, any more than they believed in this precious cousinship, but everyone pretended to believe it. The fishing had been difficult for some days, and so long as they were working on that deep bed, there would be no time for outside distractions. Moreover, Mustafa had set the tone by treating the "cousin" as one of the team. Just now, he was giving him advice.

"You mustn't force things," he told him. "As soon as you feel too heavy, and your ears are buzzing too much, let Berduk take your place. In a few days, you'll be able to pay him back for helping you out."

Stavros did not understand, but Berduk was on the alert.

"Don't worry," he said to Mustafa. "I'll take care of him. Didn't I train Turhan all right? Didn't I make a first-class diver out of him?"

"Yes, I must admit that you did," said Mustafa, and the insensitive Berduk for a moment looked anxious at the memory of Turhan's swollen face. "Both of you can take an extra half-hour's rest at noon," Mustafa went on.

"No need," Berduk growled. "The cousin is strong enough, I give you my word." He wanted no special treatment for the Greek, while Turhan stayed at home, hurt.

"Bah!" Mustafa protested. "Soon everything will be much easier. A firm in Izmir has suggested I fit the boat with a trawl. No more diving, lads. The trawl will dredge the bottom for you."

"What?" said the divers, clustering round. "What about us? What will happen to us?"

Mustafa frowned.

"You'd better make up your minds what you really want! You grouse all the time because we're not properly equipped. So I want to get us properly equipped, and you're still not satisfied! I'll still need men to handle the trawl."

"Hefty types like Berduk, perhaps," one of them grumbled, "but I might as well give up now!"

"We're not there yet," said Mustafa. "There's no trawl today, so let's get going!"

Berduk was sullen with Stavros until they reached the diving site, staying in a corner muttering with Husseyin.

To the boy's great surprise, for he had not understood Mustafa's instructions, Berduk rowed the dinghy, and was then the first to dive. The rhythm of work was quickly established, as though the two of them, the man and the boy, had been diving together for months.

When it was his turn, Stavros dived without a moment's hesitation. Berduk, apart from his outbursts of fury, was a hard but straightforward man. Stavros felt sure that he would soon notice any threatening gesture or look that might spell danger. There was nothing subtle about Berduk. He very quickly stopped watching him. In any case, the work was hard, and each depended on the other, so all hostilities were suspended.

When they came back to the caique at noon, Mustafa asked, "Did everything go all right?"

"Yeah," said Berduk.

"Did the cousin make out all right?"

"Yeah."

"You don't sound too sure."

"Me? Oh yes, I'm quite sure. That's true, isn't it, cousin, we get on well together?"

Berduk slapped Stavros hard across the shoulders, and the boy looked at him, surprised.

"Hey, not so hard!" he said, frowning.

"I see that the cousin isn't quite so easy to manage as Turhan!" Mustafa said, laughing.

Berduk shrugged his shoulders, and went to join Husseyin.

"How did it go?" Husseyin asked in his turn.

"As you see."

"I thought you meant to . . . Has Allah counseled caution through my lips?"

The veins on Berduk's temples swelled.

"It's nothing to do with you, or with Allah either. I can't do anything against this boy. I don't know whether he's Turhan or the other one. No, I just don't know any more . . ."

"But . . ." Husseyin began.

"Yes, I know. You're going to tell me that I saw Turhan yesterday evening, in Ismet's house; and that this one is the Greek. But I can't touch him any more, can't you understand? I set out once to sort him out, and it was Turhan I beat up with my fists! It might happen again . . ."

"Allah has sent you a salutary doubt. I never approved your plans. If you want to get rid of the Greek, there's nothing to stop you handing him over to the police."

"And it might be Turhan who went to prison. Now listen to me. When I hit the Greek, I hit Turhan and I hit myself at the same time. Myself, do you understand?"

He beat his chest with his fists.

Then in a low voice he said, "Turhan will never dive again. That's what I've done with my fists!"

"Who told you that?"

"I heard that nurse talking about it to Ismet."

"A woman's words . . ."

"Are like a bottle thrown into the sea, I know. But that one doesn't open her mouth for nothing, I can tell you!"

Husseyin sneered. "So there you are, condemned to diving with a Greek!"

"I don't know any more if he's really Greek. He trusts me. If he was Greek, he'd be afraid of me. And he looks so like Turhan . . ."

"Turhan doesn't wear a cross round his neck," said Husseyin scornfully.

"Now how can you be so sure of that? One thing certain is that it was round Turhan's neck when I snatched it off that night; or maybe it's not Turhan but the Greek with his face bandaged in Ismet's house!"

Berduk had never thought so much in all his life. His ideas were revolving like the propeller of the caique, and each turn took him further away from the dangerous shores to which his rancor had led him.

When the boat came back to port, as night was falling, Stavros had to admit that he was less exhausted than he had been the day before. He did not know whether to put this down to further practice, or to the tablets, or to Berduk's kindnesses. For he had to admit that Berduk had shown great generosity. He had dived more than his share, and Stavros could not help feeling a certain regard for him. The man was a tireless worker.

Turhan was waiting on the quay, a familiar shape, a bruised face, waiting for Berduk, presumably. Stavros smiled at him.

"Good evening," he said. "Do you feel better?"

"Yes," said Turhan.

As Stavros went on his way, Turhan ran after him.

"Hey! Wait for me!"

Stavros turned round. Facing the setting sun, Turhan was looking at him with eyes full of goodwill. "I can't keep up a grudge against him," thought Stavros, "not even for that idiotic game in which he stole my place!"

"Come to the Halkevi," said Turhan. "Meral wants to see you."

"Oh, good. I'll come."

Meral was looking out for them.

"I see the day passed without any excitements," she said. "Less tired than yesterday? You took my tablets?"

"One, this morning."

"Take another tonight. Otherwise, no threats?"

"No. It's hard work. We had no time to think of personal affairs."

They spoke in English, and as Turhan could not understand, he went off to watch the Ping-Pong players in the other room.

"I wanted you to come so that I could ask for your help," Meral told Stavros. "Do you really mean to go on diving for a while with Mustafa?"

"Yes, I told you I did. I've upset everyone's ideas, but now I've started, I want to get everything sorted out before I go home."

"You can."

"How?"

"By going on diving for as long as it takes Turhan to learn another trade. I phoned my father at Izmir. He has business connections there, and he could get Turhan a job as a radio operator on board ship. But Turhan will need two or three months to learn how to handle the controls and the morse code."

"Three months! Agreed."

"Perhaps you think I'm asking too much."

"No. I only think you wouldn't approve of diving the way Mustafa does it."

"That's true. These archaic methods are unworthy of a country that wants to modernize itself. If it were only up to me . . ."

"You'd leave the sponges at the bottom of the sea! And long live artificial sponges!"

Stavros laughed.

"That's not the whole of it," he said. "I am rather tired in spite of your tablets. I'm going off to bed, crossing my fingers that the police forget me for three months."

Meral smiled.

"I'll only keep you a moment longer. I wouldn't have asked you about this plan if I'd thought there was any danger of you going to prison. I've had a letter from your uncle in reply to the one you asked me to write, and he's sent your passport. He advises you to go to Izmir to see the Greek consul to put things right. I think the sooner you go, the better. Turhan could go with you, and I'll pay your expenses, for both of you."

Stavros smiled.

"You foresee everything, don't you?" he said. "Perhaps you could tell me then what I will be in three months? A superannuated sponge diver or a corpse eaten by crabs?"

"You told me that Berduk . . ."

"I was only joking. You take Turhan's affairs so much to heart."

"One of my jobs is social assistance," said Meral with dignity.

"I know," said Stavros gently. "I've already profited from your services: soup, sandals and pills. Tell me, would it be rude of me to ask how old you are?"

"No," said Meral, somewhat confused. "I'm twenty. Why?"

"You have the knowledge and the wisdom of a centenarian! And now, grandmother, may I be allowed to go to bed? Tomorrow, I go diving, you've already decided that, haven't you?"

Meral looked shocked.

"Oh! You made that decision yourself," she said. "All by yourself. I only . . ."

"Only exploited it," Stavros finished for her.

Since Meral did not seem to understand that he was joking, he added with a sudden seriousness, "I'm glad you did, Meral. I'm even grateful to you, because you only ask help from a friend, and it's very cheering, you know, to have someone who treats you like a friend."

Without waiting for a reply, he went out of the Halkevi. Outside, the lamps of the town were alight. Suddenly the exhaustion of the whole day overwhelmed him. The way back to his bed on the open hillside seemed longer than it had ever done before.

11

THE AMPHORA

The days and the weeks went by. They seemed endless. Mustafa had used the enforced holiday of the divers while the engine was being repaired as an excuse for canceling their weekly day off.

Three weeks had gone by, to be exact. Three weeks on end fishing with an adamant Berduk, who demanded an endurance from his team-mate to match his own. The kindnesses of the first day were over and done with. Stavros had to keep at it until he collapsed on the thwart from the strain, all his willpower gone. Three weeks of this turned him into Berduk's submissive companion: a trusted workmate, however, whom the man had rescued from the water on the two occasions when he was unable to surface by himself.

In three weeks they had reached the point when the Greek and the huge Turk helped and supported each other like two convicts chained together. Berduk had found another Turhan, with an overwhelming resemblance to the real one and the same courage, endurance, willpower, and pliability. For Stavros, just like Turhan before him, had become a slave whom Berduk was molding to his own standards. Stavros was too busy forcing more each day from his dog-tired body to have any mind for rebellion.

From time to time, sitting at the table in the café with Berduk and the other divers, the thought of his passport came into his mind. His illegal position was a luxury he could not afford without involving Turhan in some risk. Yet he had no time to go to Izmir, which could have been a thousand miles away so far as he was concerned. Fortunately, no policeman, however much of a busybody, could possibly suspect that the boy slumped in a chair, drinking a harmless syrup, like any other Turk, was in fact a Greek.

Three weeks without a sight of ungrateful Turhan, without a word from Meral. The Halkevi was too far away.

Sometimes a spark of satisfaction gleamed in Berduk's eyes. The bear was dancing so well to his command, and without grumbling. Stavros did not mind. For him, Berduk was now the strong sure hand that was stretched out to him as he surfaced, the vigorous body that had twice dived to save him when he had given up the struggle and let himself drift with the water.

At last the sponge bed was worked out. Mustafa decided to move to another nearer the coast, and now the diving became a sort of game, only fifteen feet down. Through the green transparency of the water, it was possible to choose a sponge from the surface, before diving straight down to it, trident in hand.

Stavros emerged now from his stupor. His curiosity, and his appetite for life returned. He set out again on his discoveries, but one thing remained the same: the reciprocal respect that linked him to Berduk and was the pledge of truce. For there could be no mistake: although Berduk still enjoyed making the bear dance, he also appreciated its quality.

The men, less exhausted, found energy to start asserting

their rights again, demanding to know how long it was to go
on, working like this without a single day off. Six weeks, Mustafa told them, to make up for the days lost while the engine
was out of action. And nothing could make him change his
mind. So they began another three week stint.

Stavros turned it into a sort of holiday, after the terrible
three weeks of the apprenticeship he had just completed. At
noon, instead of sleeping on deck with the others, he dived
from the caique, amusing himself by swimming and exploring
under water.

One day, on a reconnaissance that had taken him quite a
distance from the caique, he discovered in a jumble of debris a
slim shape that he recognized as the tip of an amphora. He
began to loosen it, patiently and carefully, and discovered that
it was indeed an antique amphora. Judging by the slenderness
of its shape it was a Greek amphora—a two-handed vessel that
had once held wine or oil. Touching this piece of pottery encrusted with sea parasites, Stavros remembered his own country
again, and the beauty of his island, Rhodes, luxuriant with hibiscus and roses. He suddenly realized that he had begun to believe that Turkey had become his home.

After this, he gave himself the right to be Greek for one
hour each day. As soon as he had finished his meal, he dived
overboard, and went on with the slow and careful task of un-
covering his amphora.

"That cousin is tireless," said Mustafa, watching him.

"You're right there," said Berduk with approval, "I've
given him a hard time, and I know some who would have gone
under. But he stuck to it!"

"I've got every confidence in your ability to train the
youngsters," Mustafa said.

Kacim shook his head, his nose in his engine.

"I will never understand why that Greek puts up with it!"
he muttered.

Stavros was tolerated by the whole team. Since he said very little, for obvious reasons, the men treated him with indifference. It was only Husseyin, who knew the truth of his real nationality, who was mildly hostile.

In the evenings, the boy went along now to the Halkevi. He never saw Turhan there, not even at the Ping-Pong table. Disappointed, he slogged away with the Anglo-Turkish dictionary, and was delighted to find his mind alert once more.

Meral was wrong, he thought. Sponge diving in these present conditions was an agreeable trade. Unfortunately, Mustafa was talking of leaving this easy bed quite soon, since it would be quickly worked out, and moving to another deeper one.

"We'll be finished here in two days," he said one fine morning.

Two days would be enough for Stavros to uncover the amphora completely. He planned to bring it out of the water, and take it back to Rhodes as a souvenir of his adventure. He had at first thought that he would borrow a boat and come secretly on his first free day. But, quite apart from the fact that he felt reluctant to behave like a thief, he was afraid that he could not manage to raise the tall jar, weighted by the sand inside it, by himself. He would have to seek help.

He was apprehensive about asking a favor, and it took a great deal of courage to approach Mustafa, for it is never easy to ask for help from the opposite side. The caique was rocking in the heavy mid-day heat. The men were already asleep, huddled together in the few shady corners. Stavros went up to Mustafa, chin high, prepared for a rebuff.

He had misjudged his boss. Mustafa was astonished at first —the boy was asking for nothing less than that the boat should be moved during the customary siesta, an audacity without precedent. But that very audacity pleased him. He rubbed his chin as he looked at the boy's face impassively awaiting his decision. Stavros had believed that showing such an interest in the am-

phora would betray his nationality in the most glaring way. But
maybe Mustafa really believed that he was Turhan's cousin, for
after a while he said, "I'm not in the habit of indulging the fan-
cies of my men. But I'm pleased with you. All right, I'll bring
the caique to your amphora. After that, it's up to you to deal
with it."

He turned towards Kacim, drowsing like a watchdog beside his engine.

"Hey, Kacim! Start moving with the engine throttled
down."

Some of the men awoke at the sound of the diesel.

"Hey, Mustafa, arc we going back?"

"No. The cousin has located an amphora, and we're going
to get it."

"Ah, good! We thought . . ."

The men were not interested, and returned to their siesta.

When they reached the place, Mustafa ordered the boat to
heave to.

"How do you mean to set about it?" he asked the boy.
"You'll need a rope, I suppose. Here, this should do the trick."

"Thank you. That'll be fine."

Stavros went to Berduk, who was snoring by the stern, and
shook him awake. The man growled, out of temper at being
unexpectedly roused.

"What's the matter with you? You ill or something?"

"I need you."

"What for? It's not time for diving yet."

"I know, but I need someone really strong."

Berduk growled again, for the sake of appearance. Any
allusion to his strength was like bait to a fish: he snapped it up.

"All right, I'll come," he said as he got up. "But . . ." He
looked around, not recognizing the coastline.

"We've moved, upon my word!"

Stavros began to laugh.

"Didn't you hear the engine? We've come here to fish for an amphora. I'll go down and fasten it to this rope, and then you pull it up when I give the sign. Agreed?"

Stavros' Turkish was not perfect, but Berduk had grown accustomed to his jargon.

"Agreed!" he said.

He took one end of the rope and wound it round his wrist.

"Now you can go."

Stavros dived. When he had knotted the rope round the two handles of the amphora, he surfaced again.

"Go ahead now. But carefully, very carefully."

He dived again to watch the operation. Above him Berduk pulled in the rope, inch by inch.

"You can go quicker now," said Stavros, coming up to fill his lungs with fresh air.

"Make up your mind!" growled Berduk. "Fast, slow, fast, slow!"

He was determined to show that there was a limit to his helpfulness.

"It's not exactly light, either," he added.

"Hold on, I'll help you."

Stavros went down again, but as the amphora was lifted, he discovered another cause for anxiety. It was even heavier, once it was out of the water.

"Wait a minute," he shouted to Berduk. "The handles may break. Throw me another rope!"

Mustafa let one down and Stavros knotted it round the belly of the amphora.

"Go ahead," he said. "And be sure to pull the two ropes together. And go slow!"

He was anxious in case the amphora should knock against the hull of the boat.

"Slowly . . . slowly . . ." he repeated.

"For heavens' sake! No one could go slower!" grumbled Berduk.

"Here, cousin, catch this buoy," said Mustafa. "Try to slide it between the amphora and the hull."

Stavros took advantage of the caique's slight list to put the protective buffer in place. When he was satisfied, he swam away from the boat to watch from a distance.

The rail was crowded. Most of the men, roused from sleep by the sound of voices and drawn by curiosity, had come to watch the rescue. Soon they were all joining in, some pulling on the second rope, others encouraging them with good advice.

For a second Stavros, at first surprised, was nearly overcome by laughter at the sight of this mob, whom he had believed to be so dangerous, now working so eagerly on his behalf. He was quickly ashamed of his mirth. At least three of them knew he was Greek, and there were certainly many others who were pretty sure of it. There was nothing at all laughable about their goodwill; on the contrary, it was cheering.

He swam to the caique, climbed on board, and reached the deck just as the amphora came level with the rail. It was even more beautiful than it had looked on the seabed, slender and elegant, and the fact that it had been almost entirely covered with sand had protected it from damage.

"That's a fine catch," said Mustafa. "You'll be able to sell it to a barber for a very good price."

That was as good as telling Stavros the amphora was his, and the boy was pleased.

"You don't often see them as well preserved as that," said Berduk.

Stavros turned to him.

"Thank you," he said. "And thank you, everyone. Without you, it might perhaps have stayed on the bottom."

"Would have, you mean," Berduk burst out, "I don't see

you lifting it by yourself. It's some weight, I can tell you!"

When everyone had gone back to sleep, their curiosity satisfied, Stavros began emptying the sand that filled the amphora. He spent the rest of his siesta on this task, for when he had washed it for the last time by swilling it out with bucketfuls of water, it was time to start work again.

There was nothing to do that evening but go straight back to his lair. The amphora was heavy and cumbersome, difficult to carry alone. He asked Berduk to lash it to his back. All the way home, people stared. Children followed him, and men passing by turned round for another look.

"Hey! Where are you going with that?" they shouted after him.

He made a vague gesture they could interpret how they liked. Once he had reached the hillside, he felt a deep sense of relief. He had been afraid of getting caught by a possible buyer, or even by the police. He wondered if he really had the right to claim ownership of an antiquity.

When he reached the foot of the wall, he was home. The amphora did not look out of place among these stones. It was just possible that the mason who put the stones in place was a neighbor of the potter who had turned the amphora on his wheel. He gazed at his treasure with satisfaction. There was silence all around him: it was the hour when the wind held its breath, and even the waves at the foot of the hills seemed to hesitate before surging back. The sun had set, leaving only a reflected glow that turned everything to copper before yielding to the gray shadows of the night. Stavros lay dreaming.

He heard footsteps climbing the hill and sat up, surprised. It was Turhan. Stavros leaped to his feet, torn between pleasure and resentment. It was four weeks since Turhan had shown any sign of life, and there was no particular reason why he should come now, unless Meral had asked him to bring another message.

"Good evening," the young Turk said.

"Good evening."

Turhan was not a talkative boy. He just stood there, awkward and silent as always. He was already regretting that Meral had persuaded him to come.

"How's that?" she had said when she heard that he had not seen the Greek since that famous evening when he went to find him at the port. "Couldn't you try to get to know him? After all, you owe him quite a lot, don't you?"

Always pliable, Turhan had agreed, much as he had agreed to study morse and radio technique, and earlier on to join Mustafa's crew. Up to this time, his life had always been arranged for him by others: and he always took on any task suggested to him with an honesty of purpose beyond all question, even when, as now, he wished he were not so submissive.

He had found it extremely difficult to go back to his studies after a three-year break: three years during which his memory and his intelligence had been reduced to a minimum. Yet even that was nothing to the difficulty of climbing that hill. Berduk's everlasting tirade against the Greek had confused any ideas he himself might have had on the subject. Left alone, he would have waited until he met Stavros again by chance. But he had been ordered a month's holiday, to recover fully from the physical exhaustion that had pulled him down; and this had in some measure cleared his mind of the confusion which held him back from making the first approach.

For the moment Stavros didn't look as though he intended to help him out. He, too, stood still and silent. Turhan made an effort and asked, "Not too hard, the diving?"

He spoke slowly and distinctly. Meral had told him that Stavros already understood Turkish very well, but he could not bring himself to believe it, since for his part he could only speak his own language, and was finding it difficult to keep the morse code in his head.

"Not too bad, no," said Stavros. "We've left the deep bed."

The crimson light of the glowing sky lit the terra-cotta of the amphora to flame on the dark ground. Turhan went up to it.

"Where did you find it?" he asked.

"The other side of the headland, near the bed we've been fishing these last few days."

"It's beautiful."

Turhan rolled it over, then stood it upright on its pointed tip.

"Put it flat," said Stavros. "You'll break the tip."

Turhan seemed not to have understood. He was spinning the amphora like a huge top. Stavros stopped this by gripping the two handles.

"I told you to put it down!" he said.

He felt a sudden surge of anger, strengthened by the resentment born of those weeks when he had waited in vain for some sign from the other boy.

"Why did you bring it here?" Turhan asked.

"Because it's mine."

Turhan shook his head.

"No. It belongs to the Turkish authorities," he said. "You must take it to the museum."

Stavros understood, from what Turhan said, only that he denied his right to the amphora, the right that Mustafa himself had granted. For a whole week all his dreams had centered on the amphora; it had become the only thing that belonged to him. Long ago it had sunk in Greek waters; it had nothing to do with this barbarous country. Besides, if the Turks had taken the least interest in it, Mustafa and the others would certainly have claimed their share in the catch.

"It's mine," he said, "and I shall take it away with me, when I go."

"You've no right."

"No right!"

Then a flood of Greek rushed from Stavros' lips. "No right! And what right have you to this amphora? What have you done with the treasures of our civilization? Where is the tomb of King Mausolus? It was one of the seven wonders of the world, and you took its stones to make your citadel! What's left of the Temple of Artemis at Ephesus, another of the seven wonders? Nothing but a dreary swamp! At Sardis, where Croesus reigned, you've let capitals and columns crumble among the weeds. Barbarians! You are barbarians!"

It was a wonderful relief to be speaking Greek and crying Greek grievances out loud, all those grievances that were whispered about in Rhodes.

Anger made Stavros forget the columns taken from Ephesus by the Greeks of Constantinople to build their church of Saint Sophia, in the days when Constantinople was not yet Istanbul; but anger has a way of being unjust.

It stung Turhan. The distrust and malice inspired by Berduk's talk rose from the inmost recesses of his mind, and swept away any concern he had felt for the stranger. He would take the amphora himself to the museum.

"Don't touch that!" said Stavros, his voice stiff with fury, as the Turk bent to lift the tall jar.

It was the willpower of the one against the stubbornness of the other. Blinded all at once by a rage out of all proportion to the futility of its cause, Stavros threw himself on Turhan, seized him by the shoulders, and began to shake him with great violence.

"Barbarian! Dirty barbarian!" he panted. "I hate you! Do you hear, I hate you!"

Turhan did not need the meaning of the Greek words to understand the gist of it. He knew now that Berduk and the others were right, and he lashed out at Stavros in his turn.

The two boys were evenly matched. They rolled among

the bushes, locked together, spitting and scratching like angry cats. Now Turhan's fury matched that of Stavros. For each of them it was the climax of an obscure antagonism whose roots were deep. Each owed something to the other. Stavros was indebted to Turhan for his fantastic hospitality; and Turhan to Stavros for these months of respite that were going to transform his life. The Greek had needed the Turk, and the Turk needed the Greek, and, without even knowing it, that was something they could not endure. With all the unbridled violence of their young strength, they attempted to settle their debts.

They fought on, their arms and legs tangled like ropes, muscles braced, fists and teeth clenched. They rolled over the ground spiked with stones and thorn bushes, sometimes crashing against the wall, from which Stavros seemed to draw new strength, sometimes lunging down towards Bodrum, when it was Turhan who with a heave forced his enemy up the slope again.

The sun had spent its last rays, and darkness fell on the hillside, blurring all detail that might distinguish one boy from the other. Suddenly, they separated, and one of them, impossible to tell which, leaped to his feet. The sound of something rolling down the hill had caught his ear. It was the amphora. The boy rushed after it, but he was too late. The fragile pottery hit the corner of a stone and shattered with a sharp sound, its shards flying into the bushes. Stavros—for it was he—knelt down and groaned. He did not turn at the sound of Turhan's footsteps. The fight was over, and the cause of it lay there, irreparably broken.

Four hands picked up the pieces in the deepening shadows. The handles were intact, still attached to the broken neck of the jar. Greek hands had held them long ago, and now because of a Turk . . .

Stavros closed his mind to that dangerous thought. He felt wretched, as he had felt after his first day's diving, but this time it was not his body, but his spirit that failed him and caused this misery; and this was far worse than the other.

He felt a hand on his shoulder. Turhan was beside him, as silent as he was, as ashamed as he that an unspoken desire for friendship should have miscarried and turned into a fight. Stavros turned towards the other boy silhouetted against the sky.

"Aren't you going to sit down?" he said.

"That's just what I wanted to ask you—may I stay here for a while?"

"Why not?"

They sat by the wall looking towards the sea. Mechanically Stavros began to stroke the two handles of the amphora, those two handles as like each other as himself and the boy seated beside him.

Below them Bodrum was garlanded with twinkling lights, and a little way beyond, only separated from the Turkish shore by a narrow channel of sparkling water, was Kos, the Greek island.

12

NAVIGATION

The following morning Stavros was surprised to find Turhan waiting by the caique. He looked him over, but the only traces of the fight were the scratches made by the thorn bushes. Stavros smiled as he passed his hand over his own face, equally scratched. As was his custom, Turhan contented himself with the traditional "Good morning," to which Stavros replied with equal brevity. They were both still bruised, and it would take time before their faces and their spirits were finally healed. But Turhan's presence so early in the morning was promising, and Stavros drew comfort from watching the boy, who stayed on the quay until the caique rounded the jetty.

He was there again in the evening, and took charge at once.

"Where do you want to go? To the Halkevi?"

"Oh, no," said Stavros.

He was worn out after a day of diving in deep water, and once again it was beyond his strength to go to the Halkevi, where, whatever he did, he would be required to make some effort.

Turhan did not insist, but led him to one of the little cafés that he knew. He felt somewhat ill at ease because he could

offer nothing more than Berduk had, but he could not take
Stavros to his home, where Ismet still kept unfailing guard, and
he could think of nowhere else.

The sight of Stavros slumped in his chair, drinking the traditional *ayran,* was enough to set his mind whirling with questions. He wondered why the Greek had accepted such hard
work, for he could have sworn that it was not solely on his own
behalf; and why he had remained in Turkey, and what he did
in Rhodes. His hands were not those of a real fisherman.

He asked none of these things, for his curiosity was not
yet strong enough to break down his instinctive reserve. He
knew moreover that after a day on Mustafa's caique, a diver
would hardly feel like talking. It was just about enough to listen to endless and trivial gossip. At least Stavros did not run
this risk; his knowledge of Turkish was still too limited for him
to get involved in the discussions going on at the neighboring
tables. Listening to these, Turhan discovered that he was no
longer able to remain uncritical. He noticed contradictions,
prejudices, exaggerations. Suddenly he was irritated by the up-
roar of voices and felt stifled by the atmosphere of the room.

"Come," he said abruptly to Stavros.

Since yesterday evening, a new feeling of sympathy had
grown up between himself and Stavros, and he was anxious
that nothing should be allowed to spoil it. He led Stavros back
to the port, and they sat in the open air watching the sea, while
the crests of the surging waves, turned to copper by the last
fiery glow of the setting sun, were extinguished one by one as
darkness came down. The following evening they returned to
the same place, and each drew courage to face the coming day
from the time spent together, Stavros for his exhausted body
and Turhan for his divided mind.

One day a storm brought the caique in earlier than had
been planned. Turhan was waiting. Just as Stavros set foot on

the quayside there was a cloudburst, so there was no question of staying outside. Turhan wondered if he must resign himself to returning to the café, but then he looked towards the castle of Saint Peter whose walls stood out against the clouded sky.

"Come," said Turhan.

He dragged Stavros to the narrow rocky path leading to the fortress. The keeper let the two boys in, and Turhan led his companion across huge courtyards swept by squalls of warm rain. He dived into a small building which Stavros discovered to be the ancient chapel of the Knights. The interior had been turned into a museum, a museum devoted to antique amphoras taken from the sea. Each one of them, supported on a metal stand, outlined its elegant shape against a light-colored panel.

"Look," said Turhan.

Stavros dried his dripping face. It was the first time that either of them had made any allusion to the subject of their quarrel. He no longer felt any bitterness about it, and now his mind experienced only pleasure at seeing the deference paid to Greek art in this museum. His amphora, if it had survived, would not have been out of place here.

He stroked the curve of one of them.

"Please do not touch," said the keeper, who had followed them.

"And what's more, they're well looked after," he thought, with pride.

They spent the next hour prowling round the little chapel, imprisoned by the storm still raging outside. In the end they were forced to leave, for the keeper showed every sign of wishing to lock the door, and dusk was coming on earlier than usual.

That night, Stavros, sleeping under a dinghy turned bottom up on the caique, dreamed that the storm was driving his trireme on to a reef. He sank, and hundreds of amphoras sank with him. He lay on a bed of sand, and as far as he could see, amphoras were pouring full-bodied Greek wine until the whole sea turned red.

"Hey! You under there! Are you awake? What a place to sleep! Be sure to make yourself at home!"

It was Mustafa's voice. The clouds were scudding in the wind, and the caique gleamed purple in the light of the rising sun. Another day's diving had begun.

At dawn, two days later, Stavros was busy washing as fast as he could when he heard the sound of footsteps pounding up the hillside. He turned round, astonished. It could only be Turhan, but why was he coming at this hour? It was indeed Turhan, breathless and anxious.

"Is your passport in order?" he asked.

"No. Why?"

"The police are looking for you."

"How do you know?"

"I reached the caique the same time as the police. They asked Mustafa for the Greek who was diving for him."

"Ah!"

"Go to Izmir and see about your passport. I'll dive in your place."

"It's a deep bed. You mustn't dive any more. You know that."

"But just for once!"

"Yes . . . maybe you're right . . . What time does the bus leave?"

"In about half an hour. But don't wait here!"

"Why not?"

"Someone might tell them where you sleep."

"Husseyin?"

Turhan evaded the question.

"Don't go into town either," he said. "Climb to the top of the hill. You can wave to the driver to stop."

These explanations were becoming too complicated for Stavros' knowledge of Turkish. Turhan drew a clumsy diagram in the soil among the bushes: the hill to climb, a path to cross, then, after a clump of pines, the road going northwards.

"Have you any money?" he said finally.

"A little."

Stavros removed one of the stones from the wall, and from this hiding place he brought his passport, and a few coins earned by selling seafish. Turhan made a face.

"The journey costs more than that," he said. "But it doesn't matter. I know the driver, he's a relative. Tell him I'll pay tomorrow. You understand?"

Stavros nodded. He repeated the sentence in Turkish.

"Goodbye, then. See you this evening," said Turhan.

"Goodbye. And be careful when you dive. Don't force it!"

Stavros watched Turhan for a while. Then, sighing, he leaped over the piece of wall and disappeared into the waste-land. It was only for Turhan's sake that he was doing this. Left to himself, he would have seen his adventure through to the very end, defied the police and risked imprisonment. But if he wanted to go on diving for sponges, he must be able to show the police that his passport was in order. This was not the moment to let Turhan down. The friendship he felt for him now took priority over the other reasons which had prompted him to take Turhan's place earlier.

When the bus announced its arrival by the sound of its overtaxed engine, Stavros had already been waiting a few minutes. He stepped forward on the stony roadway to wave to the driver, but the bus was already pulling up, as though obeying orders. It was a small bus, with about ten seats. Any travelers over that number perched on the roof with the luggage. One of them was waving.

"Stavros!"

It was Turhan.

Stavros climbed up and sat on the matting, which was the sole comfort offered by this primitive upper deck, while the bus started off with a hiccough and wheezed up the steep slope.

"What are you doing here?" said Stavros, astonished.

"There's no diving today. The police are questioning Mustafa, so he's given the fishers a day off. I'm coming to Izmir with you."

"Do you know the town?"

"I've been there once before."

Turhan's voice trembled with the continuous shaking of the bus. They jolted along the roadway, where the slanting rays of the sun threw each projecting stone into relief. The joltings, the noise, and the dust whirling in thick white spirals put an end to conversation. However, as the sharp turns on the wooded hills followed one another with nightmare frequency, Stavros yelled, "How many miles to Izmir?"

"About a hundred and sixty-five!"

"We'll never get there today!"

"We might have a bit of luck at Milas."

Milas was forty-two miles from Bodrum, and it took the little bus nearly two hours to cover them. The bit of luck did come their way, in the form of one of those collective taxis very common in Turkey, where there are still only a few cars privately owned.

The taxi already had three passengers, who squeezed up to make room for the new arrivals.

"It's not much more expensive than the bus," said Turhan. "And we'll get there quicker!"

From Milas, the road ran straight across a monotonous plain, formed by the alluvial deposits of the lazy Meander River. It was a tarred road, and the driver drove flat out. Stavros smiled, recognizing in him the similar daring of Greek drivers.

They crossed Soke, evil-smelling with its tanneries, with

much blaring of the horn, and Kusadasi, at the foot of its prom-
ontory washed by the sea, and came at last to the outskirts of
Izmir. It was nearly noon when the taxi set the boys down on
Konak Square, bordering the sea.

"So here I am at last," thought Stavros as he saw police
headquarters. "It's up to me. I can walk right past, or give myself up here!"

"Do you know where the Greek consulate is?" he asked
Turhan.

"No, but all the consulates are on that street, over there,
along the quayside. I'll go and ask."

It was nearby. Stavros' uncle had intervened, and he had
some influence. Stavros was expected. Indeed, he was scolded
for having delayed so long.

"Come back this afternoon. I'll arrange things with the
police and with the Customs," said the Consul in conclusion.

"You won't forget the permit for three months' residence,
will you?"

"Are you sure that your uncle . . ."

"My uncle gave me one year's breathing space."

"Breathing space?" The Consul looked astonished. "Are
you leading such a full life here that you're forgetting your life
in Rhodes? Looking at your clothes, however . . ."

"Is the interest of life to be measured in terms of clothes?"
Stavros asked, with a trace of impertinence.

"They could perhaps be an indication," said the Consul,
smiling.

"They may become so in my case, but at the moment I'm
only eighteen."

"And you're enjoying life here? All right then, I'll get
your permit."

Stavros was downcast when he rejoined Turhan on the
pavement.

"You've run into difficulties?" asked the young Turk.

Stavros shook his head. He would have much preferred to find a situation bristling with difficulties, but his uncle had made everything easy. He took hold of himself to ask, "Are you going to see your future boss?"

"Not now. It's too late. I'll go this afternoon."

They took the first street they came to, and found that it led into the center of the bazaar, bustling with life. Sellers of pistachio nuts, hazel nuts, almonds, apricots, raisins, figs and cakes called out to them. In their windows, proprietors of small restaurants were turning the long spindles of kebab made from thin strips of mutton, before glowing charcoal fires. A mouth-watering smell of grilled meat came to tempt the passer-by. Stavros pulled his coins out of his pocket.

"Do you think I've enough to pay for two helpings of that?" he asked Turhan.

"You certainly have. It's not expensive."

They went in, and settled themselves at a table. Stavros had enough money for two helpings of meat, two dishes of tomatoes grilled on a skewer, and two bowls of yoghurt. There was still money left for two cups of coffee, thick and fragrant Turkish coffee.

"We drink the same in Rhodes," said Stavros.

"When will you go back?"

"Not for at least three months."

"Why did you stay here? I mean, after you were ship-wrecked?"

Stavros' face, which had brightened during the meal, clouded over again.

"To see," he said curtly.

"And—have you seen?"

Turhan's eyes showed that he did not quite understand.

"Lots of things, yes."

"How will you go? Will you have enough money to pay for the journey?"

"If I want it, I will have it."

"Are you rich?"

"Yes."

"It must be very pleasant to be rich," sighed Turhan.

"Is that what you believe?"

Stavros tore off a corner of the paper cloth with nervous fingers, folding and refolding it until he had made a little boat.

"See, this boat, it's you, your life," he said to Turhan. "You are poor, you have only one sail. It takes skill to keep afloat on a straight course. But my life has been like a steamer with powerful engines, not a sail. To keep it on course is not difficult, only boring."

Turhan looked at him, surprised and unhappy, unable to believe that anyone could regret having too easy a life.

"Have you any brothers in Rhodes?" he asked, changing the subject.

"No."

"Sisters?"

"No, again."

"Your father?"

"He's dead and so is my mother."

"You're alone?"

"I've my uncle. He's rich, he's nice, he loves me. He brought me up in a glass case, sheltered from everything. But it's not only that . . . I'm too light, you understand? I'm all alone in my boat."

"Is that why you wanted to stay here?"

"Perhaps."

"My boat is loaded with people."

"You're lucky."

If Turhan had sometimes found his family a burden, he now felt deeply sorry for Stavros, all alone.

"Shall we go?" he asked, picking up the paper boat.

Stavros felt a little cheered.

"If you like."

They wandered through the busy streets until it was time to leave.

When the little bus put them down at Bodrum, late at night, two policemen were waiting for the passengers. They came up to the boys.

"Which of you is the Greek?" they demanded.

"I am," said Stavros.

"You'd better come with us," said the policeman, hustling him along.

Below, between two houses, there was a glimpse of the sea silvered by the moon. When dawn came, it would be gilded by the sun rising on the water, and the thought of seeing it again was as exciting as if he had spent long days in the prison he was now about to avoid.

When he arrived at the police station, he was suddenly frightened by the thought of going inside, with the risk of being kept there, of having to give up so many things.

"Come on, get inside!" said the policeman, hustling him again.

Stavros obeyed the summons. Shaken, he sent a grateful thought winging to his uncle, who might be too rich, but whose word had carried so much weight with the Greek Consul in Izmir.

13

THE TRIDENT

Stavros was not let off as quickly as he expected. He was kept over two hours at the police station. The customs house was alerted, and in spite of the late hour, telephone calls were exchanged with Izmir, to verify the validity of a visa of such recent date, when it was a matter of common knowledge that the boy had been in Bodrum for well over a month. Izmir confirmed that all was in order and the suspect was released.

The following day, Stavros set out for the harbor reluctantly, wondering what sort of welcome he would get on board, and what Mustafa's reaction would be. Turhan was waiting for him on the quayside, as usual.

One by one the fishermen passed the two boys and went aboard the caique. Soon only Stavros remained on the quay.

"Now then, cousin, are you coming aboard today or tomorrow?" Mustafa's voice was no different from usual.

"See you this evening," Stavros said to Turhan. He went to join the others on deck, and no one took any more notice of him than on other days.

"It's one of two things," he thought. "Either they've decided to ignore me to avoid showing their antipathy, or else they've known all the time."

He inclined towards the second explanation. It was possible that his identity might not have been known in the town, but extremely unlikely that it could have been a secret in the closed world of the caique. The problem of his acceptance by the crew must have been resolved without his having noticed it. He felt an impulse of friendship towards the men who had shown him such tolerance. He had already forgotten Husseyin's snubs and Berduk's persecution.

Up until now he had scarcely spoken to anyone other than Berduk and Mustafa. Now he began to join in the general conversation, rough talk about domestic and professional problems. Each man in turn became known, with his gentle or shrewish wife and his string of children, the parents he nearly always supported, his neighbors, and his friends. Through jokes and sly allusions, he discovered the secret sorrow of Berduk, whom he believed as safe in his strength as an elephant in its thick skin. The giant had five daughters. Five daughters, and no son to buttress his Moslem pride. He had had an adopted son, Turhan, and he had lost him.

Stavros listened and talked, but not one of the divers ever asked him a question. They pretended to forget that he was Greek; that was the most he could hope for. He had quickly understood that he must never step beyond the bounds of their neutrality.

It was a tenuous neutrality. So long as Stavros had remained apart and was content simply to dive, they had been able to forget his foreign nationality. Now that he was present all the time, with his inquisitive mind, his accent, his odd speech, he added fresh fuel to their thoughts. As soon as he left them, these thoughts took shape and were discussed in small groups.

The crew formed into two camps, one accepting Stavros without any reservation as a member of the crew, the other

consisting of the reactionaries led by Husseyin. These last ignored the fundamental reason for their hostility by asserting
that the Greek, working as he did, was stealing the job from a
Turk. They knew nothing, of course, of his agreement with
Meral.

As the days went by, the situation grew uglier. During the
hot hours of the siesta, the talk grew more violent. Stavros,
alerted by a voice raised in anger, a sentence caught by chance,
and also by the uneasy vigilance of Mustafa, realized that he
had assumed his acceptance too soon.

It all came to a head one day. It had been stormy weather
since morning, and nerves were stretched to breaking point.
Stavros stayed discreetly apart, but his presence alone was
enough to spark off a quarrel.

It was not enough for him to remain quiet. Once the discussion had started, it moved rapidly beyond control. Mustafa,
who tried to intervene, was swept aside, his authority as captain
forgotten. Berduk shouted,

"I tell you this, you don't have to ask where a lad comes
from, so long as he gets through his work."

"What! You of all people to say that! You've always said
the opposite!"

"Yes, me! Even if I have said stupid things from time to
time, I don't have to go on saying them for the rest of my life,
do I?"

"So the Greek's got hold of you, eh? Turned you over like
a squid! You're sucked dry, finished!"

"You asking for something?" Berduk lifted a heavy fist.
As though by magic a trident appeared in his opponent's hand;
but the points, directed towards Berduk's chest with no other
intention than to keep him at arm's length, touched Stavros,
who had slipped in front of Berduk.

"Why are you taking it out on Berduk?" he asked the man.

"It's me you've got a grudge against, not him. So go ahead!"

The sharp points of the trident pierced his skin and drew blood, but Stavros did not move an inch.

"Get away," growled Berduk.

"No."

The pulse in his neck was throbbing, a sign that he was frightened, but he stood firm, with his feet apart, and stared defiantly at the other man.

"Well, what are you waiting for?"

The man lowered his trident, and shrugged his shoulders. But now it was Stavros' turn to be angry, and he cried out, "I'm Greek, so what? A man is born in this place or that; what can he do about it?"

"Oh shut up, you greenhorn!" a voice shouted.

It would have taken more than that to stop the boy once he had started.

"We're all in the same boat," he said, his voice thick with fury. "We all have to work to live, whether we're Greeks or Turks. That's the only thing certain."

"Exactly," said a voice. "And there aren't too many sponges round here for the rest of us, so get back where you came from!"

"What are you talking about? It's not me fishing with Berduk, it's Turhan!"

"Turhan? What do you mean?"

"Be careful! Everyone knows what liars the Greeks are!"

"I'm not lying. I'm taking Turhan's place because he can't dive any more. He gets my share of the catch."

The men were silent while they digested this news; then a voice was lifted,

"Never known anyone take on a job like this for the sake of honor and glory!"

"That I never did!"

"You trying to make us believe all this nonsense?"

"We might ask why you're doing this fine thing for Turhan?"

"Turhan is my friend." This time he did not shout, but the warmth of his friendship was in his voice, and even the most reactionary were shaken by it. They all liked Turhan. They knew that he was loyal and courageous, and that at the age of fifteen he had become the head of his family and taken on the responsibilities of a man.

"Allah has allowed this friendship with an infidel!" said Husseyin.

"Praise be to Allah!" several voices murmured.

The crisis was over. The trident was returned to the dinghy from which a furious hand had snatched it, and the men dispersed.

"Now then, lad, what about taking a nap?" said Berduk, thumping Stavros' back. "Have to be diving quite soon now, and it's not an easy bed." Then lowering his voice he added, "You shut them up all right. A Greek has the gift of the gab, when all is said and done."

He began to laugh softly.

"When I think there was a time when I wanted to smash your face in! I could have killed you that night, I'd so taken against you!"

"You nearly killed Turhan!" Stavros murmured. "Have you forgotten?"

"Forgotten!" growled Berduk. "How could I forget, eh? That night, I beat up myself as well as the kid!" He suddenly remembered that Stavros had tried to protect him.

"Shouldn't have done that just now. He didn't scare me with his trident. I could have knocked him out with one blow, if I'd wanted to!"

"But you didn't want to," said Stavros.

"That's true. How did you know?"

"You won't ever be able to hit anyone again."

Berduk's thick black brows met in a heavy frown. "What do you know about it?" he growled.

The Greek was making him feel uneasy again, so he added, half in jest and half in earnest, "I'm still capable of shutting up anyone who talks too much!"

"No need to try," said Stavros, smiling. "I'll be quiet, I'm going to sleep."

That evening, Turhan, his eyes wide with surprise, saw his old team-mate come off the caique with his hand on Stavros' shoulder. It was as odd a sight as a bear leading its trainer on a leash.

"What did you do to tame him?" he asked a little later.

"It happened by itself," said Stavros. "We dive together, that's all."

Turhan made no reply; he could not believe it. For three years he had lived in fear of Berduk.

"You ought to see Berduk from time to time," Stavros said. "He misses you."

"Is that so?" said Turhan laughing. "I suppose he needs to sharpen his claws!"

"He's very fond of you in his own way . . . which may not be exactly gentle. At bottom, he's a decent sort."

"But . . . he wanted to kill you!"

"The other night, on that hillside, if I'd been as strong as he is, I might have killed you, you know. As for Berduk, I don't think he will ever try to kill anyone again, not when he's sober, at least. And if you give him a little of your time, maybe he won't want to drink so much *raki*."

Turhan was not keen on the idea. He had only just escaped from the tyrant, and was not eager to put himself in his hands again. Fortunately he would not have much chance of seeing Berduk for some time.

"I wanted to tell you," he said. "Tomorrow I go aboard a cargo boat for a trial period."

"What's that?"

Stavros had not understood properly.

"Come along here."

Turhan took him along the quayside and showed him a vessel of small tonnage, very spick-and-span.

"I'm going to learn how to control the radio on board. I leave tomorrow."

"And when do you come back?"

"In about three weeks."

Stavros said nothing. Life suddenly seemed as heavy to bear as it was when he was sixty feet down in the sea.

Even though he knew that his friendship with Turhan must necessarily be short, the end had come too quickly and too abruptly.

"The boat goes as far as Mersin, at the end of the south coast, and on its return trip it will go on to Izmir and Istanbul."

"And after that trial run?"

"The radio operator is leaving in a few months. I'll get the job if I'm good enough."

"You will be. Do you know what I think?"

"No."

"Strong men are needed to load cargo boats. Perhaps one day you could recommend Berduk for a job."

Berduk again!

"But . . . what about the sponges?"

"Mustafa's talking about fitting the caique with a trawl, and then he won't need so many men."

"If you think . . ."

Turhan frowned.

"You wouldn't be under Berduk's orders any more. He couldn't make you miserable again, but you could make him happy."

The idea of happiness was new to Turhan. He only knew

of a hard or a less hard life, needs that were satisfied or not. He did not know happiness.

"He didn't make me miserable," he said. "It was only that I couldn't make a move or have an idea of my own."

He discovered the truth just as he said it, and was astonished to hear himself putting it into words without having thought about it for a long time in advance. He felt free, freer than he had ever been, at the thought that he might now be the one to have a say in Berduk's life.

"Did you know that my sister Leyla is going to work with Meral?" he asked.

This seemed to have nothing to do with Berduk, yet it had. Turhan had tried out his new freedom for the first time the evening before. For the first time, he had used his power as effective head of the family, whereas before he had only exercised his duties. He had won his father's consent, and it had not been easy. Without him, Meral would never have been able to persuade Ismet to hand Leyla over to her care.

"I'm very happy for you," said Stavros. "What did your father say?"

"He had only one argument: daughters must stay at home. He doesn't realize that we, the young ones, have broken away."

"Meral has gone through that," thought Stavros. He did not understand why his friend's face had clouded over. "He can't be sorry about that victory, surely?"

"Only half a victory," Turhan was thinking. He had spent his rebellion on his sister. He had not dared, on the eve of leaving Bodrum, to bring up the difficult problem of Stavros once more. Ismet refused even to have the Greek's name mentioned. Turhan had talked of his loyalty, of the exhausting diving he had undertaken, with no thought of personal profit. All to no avail. Ismet simply growled,

"If he brings the money here, I'll throw the notes in the fire and the coins in the sea!"

And each time Turhan had answered gently, but without saying that the family had been living on Stavros' earnings for several weeks now,

"He's earning that money for me, father, and it's up to me to accept or to reject it."

Sterile discussion, in which neither changed his view.

"I'll go with you to the end of the road," Turhan suggested to Stavros.

"If you like."

Their way took them past the little cargo boat again. Berduk, planted on the quay with his hands on his hips, turned to face them.

"Good evening, lads," he said. "See that? A bit different from Mustafa's old skiff! It must be good to sail on one like that!"

"I'll be on board tomorrow," said Turhan.

"You will? It's true then? You're going to be a wireless operator?"

"Well, an apprentice to begin with."

Berduk slapped him on the back.

"Good. I'm very happy for you, lad. At least when I'm sick of the sponges I can think of you now on your good-looking boat, and it'll give me new hope. When do you get back?"

"In three weeks."

"Good luck, then. I'll try to see you when you put in again."

"Goodbye, Berduk!"

"That really is a slice of luck," Berduk was still saying, as the two boys walked away.

"I believe you're right about Berduk," said Turhan after a while.

Stavros smiled without replying. How far away they seemed, those days when he trod the sponges under the triumphant eye of the giant Turk.

14

THE ACCIDENT

Bodrum without Turhan was not much more than a prison.

On the caique, Stavros once more kept himself apart. The best way of avoiding quarrels was obviously to let everyone forget him. His hope of being simply accepted as one of the divers had gone when the point of the trident touched his chest. He'd had one victory only—Berduk.

At the Halkevi, Meral, in her turn, treated him like a stranger, and with such coldness that he could only suppose she regretted having gone too far too soon in the way of friendship. Stavros had tried to break the ice by teasing her.

"You've succeeded in rescuing Leyla from the paternal claws. Bravo!"

"I didn't. It was Turhan," she replied curtly. Stavros did not persist. Possibly Meral did not enjoy joking, or maybe he had hurt her by something he'd said earlier. In fact, Meral's attitude had a more serious cause. Stavros discovered what it was all about a fortnight later, when he was beginning to look forward to Turhan's return.

"When do you expect to go back to Rhodes?" she asked him one evening.

"But . . . Turhan has not finished his apprenticeship yet."

"He earns a little as a probationer. He can make do with what he gets now."

"In other words, you've no more use for me."

Stavros spoke bitterly, and Meral's voice was cold when she replied, "Your passport is in order. There's nothing to keep you here."

Stavros frowned. He emptied his pockets with an angry movement, saying,

"What money do I use for my return ticket? I expected to earn it sponge-diving as soon as Turhan didn't need my help any more."

Meral's face was contemptuous.

"Do you really think you need go to all that trouble? A word to your uncle, and you could have as much money as you want."

So that was it. Meral had learned that his uncle was wealthy.

"Is that what he told you to tell me? Have you been writing to him again?"

"No. But my father works in the customs house at Izmir. Your passport made quite a stir there. Your uncle's name was enough to smooth over several difficulties that might have landed you in trouble."

"I know, but that was nothing to do with me. I didn't choose to have a wealthy uncle. What I did choose was to stay here, with or without a passport, and to dive for sponges. And I shall go on for as long as necessary, whether you like it or not. You should never have suggested that arrangement if you didn't want it. I won't break it, you can count on that!"

Stavros' voice was angry. His uncle's wealth upset everything, even here.

He stalked off. Meral took him for a spoiled boy who had run away from home: and that's exactly what he was. At the end of his year of rebellion, he would go back to his secure background. He wondered whether he would find it easy to go home, now that he had broken away and seized life with both hands. He decided that Meral was wrong. This escapade, if it were an escapade, was something quite different from the whim of a spoiled child.

He slept badly that night, and went aboard the caique halfheartedly when dawn came. It was as though Meral's disapproval had finally broken his spirit, already dashed by the hostility of his fellow workers.

The day seemed even more exhausting than usual, for the heavy, stormy weather slowed the work. It was as if the tiredness that had been building up over the last weeks suddenly overwhelmed them completely.

"We'll go back," said Mustafa, with an eye on the leaden sky. "And tomorrow we'll rest."

He knew how to judge the limit of endurance of his men. It was on days of this kind that accidents happened.

"At last!" they said. "No one can say we haven't earned a rest!"

Bodrum was near. Just as the caique cleared the end of the jetty, the wind freshened.

"Double the mooring ropes," said Mustafa. "There's something brewing. Put out the buoys to protect the gunwale."

Strong gusts of wind whirled across the port and the water frothed into waves. The engine was throttled down, and Mustafa began the delicate maneuver that would bring the boat alongside the wharf.

"We'll need those buoys," he groaned. "Never seen anything like this! The wind's whirling us around like a straw!"

The divers were waiting for the moment to jump ashore. Stavros' glance took in a man coming along the quay with hesitant steps, guided by a little girl with very stiff black braids. It was Ismet, the blind man. Stavros had never seen him so far from his own home before. He had certainly chosen a bad day to come out. Stavros wondered what could have brought him, or who . . . perhaps Turhan's boat was due.

Stavros looked along the horizon in the hope of seeing the squat silhouette of the cargo boat. There was no vessel in sight, large or small. They had all taken shelter when the storm blew up.

When he took up his observation post by the rail again, the child had let go of her father's hand to run after a feather flying about in the moist air, lifted by sudden gusts of wind. The blind man was feeling for the edge of the quay with one foot before moving the other.

He and the caique were converging at the same point, the cleat on which Mustafa intended to fasten his mooring ropes. The caique was slightly ahead. Kacim took advantage of a sudden list of the boat to jump on to the quay.

"Pay out the rope," he called to Mustafa. "Stay where you are," he said to Ismet. The rope was secured. Kacim assessed the situation. The caique was bobbing about two yards from the quay.

"Have to tie it up shorter," he shouted. "The less rope you leave, the better she'll weather the storm. The hull won't come to any harm with all those buoys." He went towards the stern; and that was the moment the blind man chose to move forward again.

"Look out, Ismet!" Stavros shouted. "Mind the rope!"

But the blind man persisted. He had recognized the voice and refused to be warned by a Greek.

A few more steps, and he would catch his foot in the mooring. The caique tilted, and Stavros jumped. But the caique straightened abruptly, and he fell between the hull and the quay wall.

Stavros felt his chest compressed as though it were being squeezed by giant nut-crackers. A red haze blurred his sight. When the boat moved again he fell into the water below.

Ismet, on the quay, had dropped on all fours. With one
hand on the mooring rope he was calling, "Yildiz! Where are
you? Yildiz!" It was not the child, but Kacim who came to give
him a helping hand.

"I told you not to move," he grumbled.

Everything had happened so quickly that the men on
board the caique had not seen Stavros crushed. He had fallen
into the water, but, after all, he was a diver by trade. He could
find his way out.

"He hasn't come up." Berduk said suddenly, for he had
been watching the surface. "I bet you he's really hurt."

He dived in, and two others followed him. They swam
under the boat to find Stavros spread-eagled on the hull by the
swell of the water, and brought him to the surface. Kacim
helped them to hoist him on to the quay.

"I didn't see him fall," he said.

"What's the matter?" asked the blind man.

"It's a drowned man," replied Yildiz, who had taken her
father's hand again. "You'd think it was Turhan, you know, father, the other one . . ."

Ismet shuddered.

"What's happening?" he asked once more.

"But, father, I told you . . ."

"It's the Greek," said Berduk. "He got caught between the
hull and the quay."

Mustafa, who had seen nothing of the accident, leaned
over Stavros.

"Poor young lad!" he said. "How did it happen?"

"He wanted to jump and he lost his footing," a voice said.

"Why was he in such a hurry?"

"He saw that Ismet was going to catch his foot in the
mooring rope. I was going to jump as well. It all happened so
quickly."

One by one the divers left the boat and gathered on the

quay. They all headed straight for the unconscious boy.

"This time, I don't know what to do," said Kacim. "Better not to touch him in case there's internal injury."

"We'll call the doctor," said Mustafa.

"Not certain he'll be there. It's the day for his rounds in the coastal villages. I know because the day my wife . . ."

"Not worth it," said Berduk. "He's coming round. A Greek's like a cat—he's got at least nine lives!"

There was no animosity in his voice: instead, almost a note of admiration.

Stavros opened his eyes and groaned, as he moved his hands to his chest.

"Now then, cousin, what's wrong?" Mustafa asked him.

"There may be some ribs broken," said Kacim. "Did the boat crush him badly?"

"It's difficult to know," said Berduk. "I think he was near one of the buoys. That was lucky; it must have taken some of the weight."

A gust of wind lifted the dust on the quayside, and made Stavros cough, so that he groaned again. A peal of thunder rumbled behind the hills.

"We can't stay here like this, doing nothing," grumbled Berduk. "It'll be pouring with rain soon, and there's no point in us all getting wet. Where shall we take him?"

"Where does he sleep usually?" asked Mustafa.

"Up there, in the open air, on the hillside. He can't do that tonight."

"I thought he lodged with you, Ismet," said Mustafa, turning to the blind man.

Two policemen came up, attracted by the crowd.

"What's the matter?" they asked in their turn, enabling Ismet to avoid the embarrassing question.

"It's the Greek!" said one of them.

"What has happened to him?"

Stavros sat up, his face strained with the effort.

"Nothing," he said. "I took an unwanted bath!"

"Move on, then! What are you all waiting for? The rain?"

A few heavy drops were already falling.

"Bring him to my house," said Ismet. "Turhan's bed is empty. He can rest there. Come, Yildiz."

"We're going back home, father?"

"Yes."

"He isn't drowned, you know, that other Turhan. But he's dreadfully pale."

The little girl bit her lip. Her father saw nothing but he felt her small hand grip his, and he scolded.

"Come on now, hurry up! You know quite well that it's begun to rain."

"Will you be able to walk?" Mustafa asked Stavros.

"I think so."

If he took only shallow breaths, the pain lessened. He preferred to try to walk, rather than lie there on the ground, with the dust making him cough. Berduk helped the boy to stand up.

"I'll go with you," said Kacim. "There ought to be two of us, in case the cousin takes a turn for the worse."

He supported Stavros beneath his other arm.

"How's it going, boy?"

"All right."

After all these weeks of struggling to stand on his own, Stavros gave in. He was defeated, body and spirit, ready to give way to anyone who would take care of him. He clung to Berduk, as he had clung to the cask the night he was shipwrecked.

He was not conscious of his arrival in Ismet's house. Worn out by the effort he had made in climbing the narrow streets, he had fainted in the men's arms. They carried him into Turhan's bedroom, and laid him on the mattress.

"Hey, little girl!" Kacim called, seeing a child looking curiously round the door. "Do you know Meral, the nurse at the Halkevi?"

The child nodded her head.

"Go as fast as you can, and bring her here. Tell her to let the doctor know, if he's there. Off with you!"

Then the blind man came in, and leaned against the door frame.

"How is he?" he asked.

"Not too good," said Berduk. "Haven't often seen a kid as brave as this one. We should have carried him from the harbor. He was as strained as a mooring rope in bad weather, all the way here."

Ismet said nothing. He went up to the bed, and leaned over it. His fingers traveled over the face of the injured boy. A slight uneasiness clouded his own, for now he found the resemblance he had denied on that first day.

"Meral is coming at once," the little messenger announced breathlessly, on her return.

"That's good," said Ismet. "Now go and play with your sisters."

Meral appeared very quickly. She took the men aside.

"What has happened? Aissa couldn't tell me."

"He got crushed between the quay and the boat," said Berduk, pointing to Stavros.

"Was it you who brought him here?"

"He came on his own two feet. He only collapsed when he got here."

"A stupid accident," said Ismet. "I wasn't in any danger. There was no need for him to jump."

"Because . . ." Meral was beginning.

She went no further. She had come to look after an injured man, not to examine the causes of his accident. She pulled up his undershirt, and looked anxious when she saw that the skin was unmarked.

"His injuries must be internal," she said. "I can't do anything for him. But I've already told the doctor, and he won't be long now."

When the doctor arrived, he asked for a summary of the accident.

"Good," he said. "Now, will you all leave? There are too many people in this small room. Not you, Meral, of course."

A little later, he joined the three men waiting in the passage.

"Well?" said Berduk.

"He's recovered consciousness. Nothing serious, in my opinion. General compression of the chest, and there are certainly one or two ribs cracked. I'll look at that on the X-ray tomorrow. His bad reaction was due to exhaustion. He's been overdoing it lately, hasn't he? Always this diving! When is Mustafa going to modernize his boat?"

"He's talking about buying a trawl."

"That would be a good idea. You're all at the mercy of an accident like this one. But there's nothing seriously wrong with the boy. All he needs is a week's rest."

He turned to the blind man.

"One of your relations, I suppose? Unbelievable how much he resembles your Turhan. How is he, by the way?"

"Very well," said Ismet. "He's working as a wireless operator on a cargo boat."

"That's fine! That's one of them saved at least. If you'd listened to me earlier on, Ismet, you would still have your sight. I'd warned you of the dangers, and you're paying for your obstinacy. But at least your son will be spared, and maybe that other boy as well."

"Can we go to see him?" Berduk asked.

"Yes, but only for a short time. He must rest."

Kacim and Berduk went into the room.

"Well I'm blessed!" said Berduk, seeing Stavros welcome them with a smile. "You really did have us worried."

He began to laugh, for the doctor's diagnosis had brought him great relief.

"Three of us dived in to fish you out!" he said. "And I'll give you ten guesses who dived with me!"

Stavros lifted his eyebrows and Berduk went on,

"Husseyin! And Ismail, the one who poked you with the trident! You certainly made them change their minds about you."

He leaned towards Stavros and said, "Tell me cousin, how do you set about winning us all over like this, one after the other? I can't say it's because of your face, in fact I'd say that goes against you. As though you were making fun of us all by looking so exactly like one of our own lads. So how . . . ?"

"I haven't done anything at all," said Stavros. "We just know each other better, that's all."

He looked at Meral, standing in a corner of the dark little room, and added, "To know each other, that's all there is to it. Not to believe in appearances, or preconceived ideas."

Berduk pushed back his cap and scratched his head.

"You're probably right, as always. Well, we'll leave you now. The others will be waiting for news. We'll go and put their minds at rest. Coming, Kacim?"

When the two men had gone, Stavros struggled to get up.

"What are you doing?" Meral asked sternly.

"I'll be off. It would be better."

"Out of the question. Where would you go, in this weather?"

"It doesn't look as though it will rain much."

"Not yet. There've only been a few drops. But the storm's

moving around. It won't be much longer before it breaks."

"I can't stay with Ismet, you know quite well I can't. He's never allowed me inside his house."

Meral forced Stavros to lie down again.

"It was Ismet himself who told them to bring you here, apparently. Is that enough to put your mind at ease?"

Meral's voice seemed to have recovered its former warmth.

"I think I'll let myself believe it," Stavros murmured. He thought about the kindness with which he was being treated. Berduk's concern, the help of Husseyin and Ismail, those reactionaries! He closed his eyes and curled up like a drowsy cat in the narrow bed. The pain was ebbing under the influence of the sedative the doctor had given him.

"That's right," said Meral. "Go to sleep now, I'll look in again on my way home this evening."

"I'm behaving like a spoiled child, aren't I?" Stavros murmured, feeling his mind and his body unable to make the slightest effort.

Meral laughed softly.

"That's not what your friends say," she said. "Now have a good sleep. See you later . . . cousin!"

15

THE
LAST
BASTION

Stavros awoke the following morning to a feeling of complete peace. He let himself drift, his muscles relaxed, his grateful thoughts going to the doctor who had secured this comfort for him. There was just a hint of pain, far away in the background, if he breathed too deeply.

A woman's face smiled from the doorway briefly. It was like a vision from another life. Stavros went back several years into a world where he was still a child in his mother's care. He closed his mind to the present so as to enjoy that pleasant illusion for as long as possible.

Later in the morning he heard the sound of a familiar voice. His heart gave a leap, and he called out, without daring to believe it, "Turhan!"

"Stavros! It's true then? I saw Leyla. She told me you'd been injured, and that father had opened the door to you. What happened?"

Stavros stumbled through an account of the incident.

"You don't look very well yet," said Turhan.

"It's this sedative! I've no more energy than a sea-snail."

Turhan began to laugh.

"That really would surprise me!" he said.

"Tell me about yourself. Did you like your work?"

"Yes, very much indeed. And then some! I'm only assistant operator now, but when I'm on my own . . ." He broke off and began to laugh again.

"It's not the captain, it's the radio operator who's the master of the ship," Turhan continued.

"How's that?"

"Well, without him, the boat is lost. No more messages. And if she needs help, no one to send for it."

Stavros smiled. He wanted to say, "It's not quite as simple as that!" but saw no point in upsetting Turhan's satisfaction. Lucky Turhan, to be so happy. Stavros thought for a moment of his own muddled future, but did not dwell upon it. Each day could take care of itself. He had enough to do, trying to struggle with this extraordinary lethargy. Making a great effort, he swung his feet to the ground.

"He must not get up," said a gentle voice from the door. "Meral has forbidden it."

The mother was watching discreetly over the invalid who had been put into her care. Stavros turned his head towards her. For the second time, the memory of his own mother returned with such strength that it flooded his mind.

"I'm caught in the past like a fish in the meshes of a net!"

He had murmured the phrase in Greek so Turhan caught only the desolation in his voice.

"What is it?" he said. "Do you feel bad?"

"I feel weak," said Stavros. "I feel that I would like to run home to my uncle and cry out to him, 'Protect me. Take me back quickly, and look after me.' "

Turhan looked at Stavros in astonishment.

"But I don't want to, do you understand? I don't want to!" cried Stavros.

His agitated breathing brought back the pain in his chest, and he clenched his fist.

"I thought you had no more energy," Turhan said.

Stavros began to laugh.

"I feel better," he admitted.

There was a step in the passage.

"Are you there, Turhan?"

"Yes, father."

"Will you ask the Greek if he will share our meal?"

Turhan looked at Stavros, a question in his eyes.

"With pleasure," said the Greek.

The blind man winced, as he did each time he heard the boy's voice.

Stavros watched him leave with an apprehensive face. Staying in Bodrum was rather like going of his own free will into a lion's den. He had been all but torn to pieces at first, then his presence had been tolerated, and now some had ended by feeling affection for him. There remained Ismet . . .

The meal brought the man and the two boys together. The girls were invisible, and the mother served the meal in silence.

"What sponge bed are you working on?" asked Turhan, to break the silence.

Ismet gave Stavros no time to reply. He intervened, saying, "Greek, Turhan has told me that you wanted to give him the money you earned. That money is yours. We don't want any part of it."

So Turhan had not told him that the money had already been handed over. Stavros thought for a moment before he said gently, "Some weeks ago, Turhan said to me 'Let's play a game. I will be Stavros. You will be Turhan.' So it is Turhan who dived and who earned that money."

"What's all this about?" Ismet grumbled. "Turhan, will you kindly explain . . ."

Turhan's face reddened. Berduk wasn't wrong when he said the Greeks had crafty tongues. That way of putting things . . .

"Stavros has spoken the truth," he acknowledged. "But I had thought the game finished a long time ago."

"Ridiculous!" said Ismet. "How could a Greek pass for a Turk?"

"We look very much like each other, you know," Stavros said quietly. "If you could see me, when I come back from a day's fishing, I don't think you would be able to say whether it was your son or me."

"Why did you play this game? What did you expect to gain from it?"

"I've already gained a great deal. The first day, most of Mustafa's men would have liked to throw me into the sea, with my arms and legs tied together. Yesterday, when I fell, three of them dived in to save me: Berduk, Husseyin and Ismail. You know them?"

"Yes," Ismet admitted. "What then? How much better off does that make you? If you had returned to your own home, that first day, no one would have wanted to throw you into the sea then, or fish you out now."

Stavros clenched his fists. Words crowded into his mind, jostled each other, fed on his anger.

"I am eighteen years old," he snarled. "I have every intention of leading my own life, and not the one people have led before me. I refuse to hate because they hated. I want to judge everything for myself. I stayed here because I was curious. I have found some friends. Would you have preferred me to take another sort of image of the Turks of Bodrum back to Rhodes? To say—they are as brutal as Berduk, as intolerant as Husseyin? Isn't it better that I should say—'I had a team-mate who was strong as only the Turks can be strong, who looked after me as though I were his son. I know a fanatical Moslem who saved my life, even though I am an infidel.' "

Stavros paused for breath, and then added in a lower voice, "That I should say 'I knew a blind man who did not like the Greeks, yet he opened his door to me when I needed shelter, and his son became my friend'?"

A silence fell in the room. Turhan, dismayed, looked from Stavros, his face tense with emotion, to Ismet, impassive, sheltered by his dead eyes. Torn between the two of them, he did not know which to dread most: the appalling anger that his father was bound to manifest sooner or later, or Stavros' precipitate exit from the house, whom he could already imagine wandering over the hillside, not yet fully restored to health.

Stavros was the first to break the silence. He murmured, his hand on his chest, which was giving him pain again, "Set your mind at rest. I am going back to Rhodes. There is nothing for me here since you refuse me the right to work any more to help Turhan . . . and since I probably can't dive any more."

"Oh!" said Turhan. "When will we see each other again?"

"You never know, maybe another storm . . ." As Turhan looked sad, Stavros added, "We are neighbors. We are bound to meet again."

The mother brought in cups of thick coffee.

"Will you come to the port with me?" Stavros asked.

"Meral has forbidden you to go out," the mother intervened in her gentle voice.

"I have to make plans for my departure."

"Meral said 'a week's rest,' " the mother repeated.

"Be silent, woman!" said Ismet.

The mother withdrew without a sound. Ismet pushed back his chair.

"You, the Greek, are my guest for a week," he said.

"But . . ." Stavros began.

"You are in no shape to travel."

"But . . ." Stavros tried again.

The veins on the blind man's temples swelled with anger.

"Who brought you up, Greek? Who told you that a boy of your age has the right to interrupt when a man is speaking to him? Did no one teach you respect for your elders? Be silent, and do as you are told; that is what every sensible father teaches his son."

A father, a son. That lecture might as well have been directed against Turhan. The lion was still roaring, but not with threats any more. Stavros found it reassuring to be scolded like that, and to hear himself being taught the basic principles of Moslem education—he who did not know how to be silent, and who believed blind obedience to be a manifestation of "deplorable passivity," as Meral would say.

Respectfully, he murmured, "I will be your guest, Ismet."

"How do you mean to get home?" Turhan asked him when they were once more in his room.

"I'll swim," said Stavros.

"Swim?"

Turhan could never get used to the crazy way Stavros conducted his affairs. He had not yet recovered from the discussion with his father, and now here he was suggesting that he swim for home!

"We go very close to the island of Kos when we round the headland," said Stavros. "I shall ask Mustafa to go in as close as he's allowed, and then I'll jump overboard. I'll easily find a boat in Kos that will take me to Rhodes."

He smiled sadly.

"It's time to go back to the big fat steamer on the well-charted course."

"You can't do that," Turhan said, speaking with unusual firmness.

"Do what? Swim as far as Kos?" asked Stavros.

"No, pilot a steamer."

Turhan hesitated, trying to find the right words. Even though Stavros spoke Turkish with assurance, Turhan was always afraid of not being understood. He took out of his pocket the little paper boat which he had kept since their trip to Izmir.

"You need to struggle against the wind, to labor with the boom, to tear your hands to pieces on the halyards."

He mimed these actions.

"But you're quite capable of ramming your steamer on a reef," he went on, "or stowing your cargo badly in a storm. You're too fond of taking risks. Later, perhaps, when you are older, and not so headstrong . . ."

Stavros' face cleared. It was remarkable how Turhan had sized things up, and he wondered how long it had taken him. He was right, of course. It was obvious that Stavros was not yet mature enough to assume the responsibilities that his uncle wanted to put on his shoulders: and there at last was the one argument that would convince him. And it was Turhan, with his slow mind, who had found it, while Stavros had been going round in circles for months, searching for the answer.

Stavros picked up the paper boat, and put it in the hollow of his palm.

"You're right," he said. "There's nothing like working on a boat to teach you the job.

"If I'm ever in trouble," he joked, "I could always send you an S.O.S."

He tapped on the wall: three short, three long, three short.

"Is that right?"

"Yes," said Turhan. "Would you like me to teach you the morse code?"

"Let's start."

Stavros was a good pupil, but he made mistakes that reduced them to helpless laughter. Pain stabbed again in Stavros' chest. All the same, when Meral arrived late that evening and spoke of going to take X-rays at the doctor's surgery, there was a storm of protest. But it needed more than that to intimidate her, and Stavros had to submit. The X-rays revealed that three ribs were badly cracked. There could be no question of swimming home.

16

RHODES

Stavros, his chest strapped with bandages, spent the following days on the caique. Even more stubborn than Meral, he had got permission to do so by insisting that boredom was bad for him. Once Turhan had set out again, it was not very amusing for someone as active as Stavros to be left alone with Ismet. And it was good to be back on the caique, warming himself in Mustafa's goodwill and the rough companionship of Berduk.

Since he was not diving, of course, he had all the time in the world to think about the problem of his return to Rhodes. His agreement with Meral had been broken by the chance of his accident, and Stavros could do no more for Turhan, for sponge-diving requires sound ribs. Fortunately, Turhan's salary would soon be increased, and Leyla was going to be earning money as well.

There still remained the problem of his return home. There were plenty of shipping lines between Izmir and the island, but Stavros was reluctant to adopt a solution that would cost money, more than ever needed at this juncture by Turhan's family. He became haunted by the island of Kos, so near and yet so far, now that he could no longer hope to reach it by swimming.

One morning, the last day of the rest imposed by the doctor, he approached Mustafa.

"Do you know of any old, abandoned boat?" he asked him.

"What for?"

"To get to Kos with. But I couldn't bring it back. That's why it would have to be old and abandoned."

"Would you be able to row with your cracked ribs?"

"I'd go slowly. I could take my time."

Mustafa rubbed his chin, and turned to Kacim.

"Hey!" he said. "You don't know of any old boat, do you?"

Kacim scratched his head with the old familiar gesture.

"I don't!"

"Well, do you know of a caique that should be in port in the next few days?"

"What a question! Doesn't it happen to be our day off tomorrow?"

"Now, that's very true! What about it then? Would you be ready for a little trip round by Kos?"

"Is the cousin leaving us?"

"He wants to."

"Agreed then, that little trip."

"And what if we went as far as Rhodes while we're at it?"

"That's all right by me."

"But . . ." Stavros began.

He held his tongue. He wondered if he would ever be able to say that word without remembering Ismet's counsel, "Be silent, and do as you are told."

"It's time I went," he thought to himself. "I'm becoming too docile!"

"But," he said the word very firmly, "you can't go as far as Rhodes."

"We can anchor at the limit of Turkish waters, and Kacim

can take you in on one of the dinghies. Isn't that so, Kacim?"

"Well, it's just that . . ." Kacim began, scratching his head desperately.

"I'm not asking you to land the cousin in the middle of the port at Rhodes. He must know some deserted creek or other."

"What deserted creek?" asked Berduk, as he climbed over the rail.

"To land the cousin on his island, tomorrow."

"So it's decided, then. You're leaving us?" said Berduk. "Count on me to put you off in your creek."

He gave his great guffaw of laughter.

"Nothing I like better than thumbing my nose at the coastguards!"

"Honestly," said Stavros. "You need only take me to Kos. It's a long way to Rhodes, and fuel is expensive."

"We'll sail there," said Mustafa. "A nice trip. We're in for a spell of fine weather at the moment. Look!"

Stavros lifted his eyes to the blue sky, then looked at his companions, who were all smiling.

"Yes, the weather's set fair," he murmured.

Mustafa had been right in his forecast. The following morning was misty, promising good weather.

"Why don't we raise anchor?" Stavros asked, since Mustafa seemed uncertain about making a start, even though both Kacim and Berduk were on board.

"We've plenty of time," Mustafa replied. "It's a long day. We'll let the mist disperse."

An hour later, when the mist had disappeared, the caique hoisted sail and headed for the south. The whole crew had turned out. They had arrived one by one, Husseyin last of all, running and grumbling,

"What an idea! Going on a trip at this hour! I thought I'd be too late!"

They were all there, but none of them paid the Greek any special attention. They just made a place for him on the rail, so that he could share their enjoyment of a dolphin leaping in their wake. But the natural reserve that kept their mouths closed and their eyes turned aside was of no importance. They had all come, that was the important thing: as it was important that Meral was on the end of the jetty to watch the caique go by.

Stavros found that he did not enjoy the prospect of leaving his companions. They had all gone through so much to reach this point. Simultaneously, for the first time in these long months, Stavros began to think of his uncle with affection. His escape from Rhodes had been an act of rebellion. He knew that now. In future, he would regard his uncle's work with more respect. Commissioning and equipping ships was a fine career, but he wanted to start, not at the top, but at the bottom.

He would go to his uncle and say, "I've a lot to learn before I join you. I am ambitious; but I want to make my own way, without the use of your money."

He would work his way up by his own efforts. He was sure he could do it. There could be nothing harder than diving sixty feet down for the first time under the critical eyes of Berduk.

"Seems to me we'd better wait a bit before we take to the dinghy," said Berduk, when the caique reached a point level with Rhodes. "Coast guards are like everyone else—at noon they want to sleep. We'll get by easier then."

"I hope all goes well," said Stavros. "I don't want to get you into any trouble."

Berduk laughed, slapping him on the back.

"Have a look at this," he said.

From a canvas bag he pulled out fishing tackle.

"As soon as we see a boat, we let ourselves drift, our rods in the water. Two fishermen in a dinghy, not bad, eh?"

Stavros started to laugh too.

"You're right there!" he said.

"This is for me, of course. You'll be all right. You'll be on your own home ground, with your own passport."

"I haven't got a passport any more."

"Did you forget it?"

"I threw it in the harbor before we set out."

"You did *what?*"

Berduk stared. Stavros smiled, thinking of Turhan, who would have said, "You really can't help it! You just have to make things difficult for yourself."

"Anyway," said Berduk, "that doesn't alter the fact that you'll be on your own ground. It'll be enough to tell them, you're Greek . . ."

"If we're caught, I won't understand Greek. I shall be Turhan, son of Ismet!"

"You'll do what?" Berduk said again.

He dimly began to understand that Stavros did not want him to run any risks that he could not share.

"Don't worry!" Berduk said. "There'll be no need to play that part again!"

He turned to Mustafa.

"Do you agree then, that we wait a bit!"

"That's all right by me. But it's six or seven miles from here to Rhodes, and you'll have time to get overheated, rowing at noon!"

"Bah!" was Berduk's only reply.

"Won't be worse than treading sponges, will it cousin?" he murmured, leaning towards Stavros. He laughed again, and Stavros endured another thump on his back.

"You know the cousin's got some ribs cracked," said Mustafa. "You can't be doing him much good, thumping him like that."

"I forgot. Have I hurt you?"

"There must be one or two ribs left in good condition. If you want to use them . . ."

Berduk laughed again. His laughter rolled along the deck of the caique, putting everyone else in good spirits.

Then it was noon. He lowered the dinghy, helped Stavros down into it, and took the oars.

"Right then, Mustafa. Don't go without me. Bodrum's too far for me to row."

"Don't worry. Take your time. While you're sweating away, we're going to have a nice long siesta! Right then, goodbye, cousin!"

"Goodbye, Mustafa. Goodbye, everyone. I'll come back one day."

"Swimming, next time?"

"Why not, if there's no other way?"

"I wouldn't put it past him!" shouted Berduk. The dinghy made off. The sea was smooth, and the rowing not too hard. The caique rocked gently, her rail lined with faces. Gradually it dwindled to a shape on the horizon, while the golden coast of the island came nearer.

Berduk had been right. The sea was deserted at this hour. Stavros guided him to a sheltered creek to the west of the town. The hull scraped the shore, and Stavros stepped out into the water.

"Well, now you're back!" said Berduk. "Where exactly is your home? In Rhodes itself?"

"Yes."

"Not too far from here?"

"Not so far as Bodrum!"

"That's true. And I've no doubt you'll find someone to give you a lift to your very doorstep!"

The waves were softly breaking on the shore, swinging the

little boat as though to anchor it permanently in the sand. Berduk let her go, his oars shipped. Stavros smiled. Berduk's reluctance to leave was worth any protestation of friendship.

"Better not hang around," he said. "No sense in tempting fate!"

"You're right, once more. So—goodbye, cousin!"

"Goodbye, Berduk—and good diving!"

"Trust me!"

Berduk pushed the dinghy into deeper water. Stavros watched him, overwhelmed by a desire to go back with him.

"Hey!" he called. "When you see Turhan . . ."

"Yes?" said Berduk, letting his oars float.

"Nothing," said Stavros.

He pulled himself together and waved his hand.

"Goodbye!"

He turned away, and walked towards the boulders encircling the creek. Berduk's voice followed him.

"Don't worry! I'll tell Turhan everything. The passport in the water, the trip in the dinghy, and all the rest. Goodbye, cousin!"

Stavros did not answer. It was an uprooting, but one that must be accepted. He climbed to the top of the rocks. Before him were the outskirts of Rhodes, the white houses, the gardens covered with hibiscus and bougainvillea. Over there, the Castle of the Knights. One day, he would show Turhan the sights of the town. He would give him a taste of Greek hospitality.

Now that he was alone, he allowed himself to look back. Berduk's small dinghy was drawing away on the sparkling sea, still linked to the coast by the narrow ripple of its wake. He was still in Greek waters, beyond which the caique waited.

Stavros sighed. One day, perhaps, the old enmities would be forgotten in friendships like that between Turhan and himself. He turned his face towards the town.

ABOUT
THE AUTHOR

Jacqueline Cervon comes from a village in Nivernais, where for several centuries her family have lived and worked as craftsmen in wood. After taking her degree in Paris, she married and lived in Djibouti in East Africa for eight years before returning to France so that her three children could be educated in a more gentle climate. Although she has now settled in the village where she was born, she enjoys traveling with her family each summer to remote and unfamiliar places.

Mme Cervon has written twelve books for children, of which *Castaway from Rhodes* is the second to be translated into English.